A Stitch in Time

By Susette Williams

Published by Family Friendly Fiction
© 2018 by Susette Williams

Dedication

Thanks to God for giving me inspiration and the desire to write; my husband, Rob, and to our six children, Delilah, Eric, Melissa, Gabrielle, Nehemiah and Nathaniel.

Chapter One

"Elizabeth Ruth Peterson, you are even more persnickety than my mother was growing up during the time of the World's Fair," said Great-grandma Mullane, her stern features buried beneath the wrinkles of age and wisdom. "If you keep turning your nose up at young suitors, you'll be too old to have children when you finally do get married. Your great-great-grandmother didn't have me until she was thirty-eight years old, and she's lucky she didn't die giving birth."

Lizzie sighed. She felt trapped in the small confines of her grandmother's dining room. Fumbling with the delicate Delaware china cup, a tiny crack visible along one portion of blue roses and scrolls, she took the last sip of her hot green tea. "I know, Grandma Mullane."

"You know that Grandma Mullane and I are just worried about you, sweetie. It's not good for anyone to be alone." Grandma Bader patted Lizzie on the shoulder.

Great-Grandma Mullane was in her early nineties, and Grandma Bader, who was only nineteen years younger, were both widowed and lived together.

Having Grandmother Bader and Great-grandmother Mullane both living in the same house made it challenging to visit either of them. One-on-one, Lizzie felt outnumbered, but double-teamed… she felt like she was under a microscope. Why had she let her mother talk her into staying with both her widowed grandmothers to keep an eye on them while she and her father were out of town? After spending a day and a half with them, she remembered why she'd left Warrensburg and moved to St. Louis—to avoid scrutiny from her family.

Christmas wasn't far away. She had to finish her shopping and wrapping presents. Right now, the thought of fighting crowds looked appealing as opposed to having the marriage discussion with her grandmothers.

"I'm only twenty-eight. I've still got plenty of time to find a husband." It wasn't like she wasn't looking. Most single men her age had already fathered children or gotten divorced, some of whom wanted nothing to do with getting married again because of their previous experience.

"Go get my mother's quilt from the cedar chest at the end of my bed," Grandma Mullane told her daughter. "I had planned to wait to give it to her until Christmas, but I think it's high time Lizzie heard the story."

Lizzie took a deep breath and forced herself to smile politely. She cleared their empty tea cups from the table and took a moment of solace as she quickly washed the few dishes and put them in the strainer on the kitchen counter.

Each step felt heavier as she made her way back to the dining room. Grandma Mullane had already spread the quilt out on the table. Wonderful. Story time. Lizzie wasn't a child anymore; she didn't need to hear stories. Not that some of her grandmothers' stories weren't entertaining. However, if they were on the topic of marriage, those stories felt more like a lecture.

She might as well get this over with. Her grandmothers would both be going to bed in a couple hours, then she could enjoy some quiet time by herself.

"So, what's the story behind the quilt?" Lizzie took her seat and watched as Grandma Mullane's frail fingers traced pieces of fabric on the quilt.

"It's a story I've only heard once before," said Grandma Bader. "But I'm going to let her tell you it in peace while I go take a long hot bath before bed."

Lucky her, she was able to escape and enjoy some quiet time by herself. Lizzie longed to do the same. Instead, she leaned her arms on the table and waited patiently for Grandma Mullane to begin her story.

"My father always said my mother spent so much time living in the past and what should have been that she nearly missed out on one of the biggest blessings in her life—me." Grandma Mullane expelled a deep breath. "My mother was a good woman, but she always had a far-a-way look in her eyes. This quilt," Grandma said, patting it, "was her memento of her youth. I'm not sure it was a good thing she kept it or not, because she could never fully move on."

"Move on from what?" Lizzie wasn't sure how any of this related to her, but the story intrigued her, and she honestly wanted to find out more.

"From the demons that haunted her." Grandma Mullane's faint smile didn't quite reach her eyes. "You see, this quilt was the story of the time she spent at the World's Fair in 1904, and of the love she never spoke about until she gave me this quilt the month before she died."

"So, she was in love with someone else?" Lizzie's heart ached for Elizabeth. "Why didn't they get married?"

"Her father didn't approve of him. You see, her father was a man of means, and he expected her to marry someone who could adequately provide for her." Grandma Mullane shrugged, her hand gently brushing across the fabric. "He didn't think this gentleman, a common laborer, would be a good match."

Lizzie's great-great-great-grandfather may have been looking out for his daughter, but he should have considered her feelings. "Why didn't they just elope?"

Grandma Mullane smiled. "They were going to." Her expression turned somber. "But something happened."

Lizzie waited a couple moments in anticipation, expecting her grandmother to continue. When she could take the silence no more, she blurted, "So what happened?

"At least you are humoring an old lady and her stories." Her grandmother laughed. "Unfortunately, their love story didn't have a happy ending. When I asked my mother why she didn't marry him instead of my father, she broke down in tears." Grandma shrugged her shoulders. "So, I never really got to find out what kept them from getting married. I do know this piece of fabric here…" She pointed to a piece of dark blue fabric in the middle of the flower petals. That was the only piece of fabric that was the same on all three of the flower patterns of the quilt. "That dark blue came from something he wore. My mother placed it there because she said he was at the center of everything in her life."

"Uh." Lizzie sighed. What happened to keep them apart? "Do you know what his name was?"

Grandma Mullane gazed at the quilt with eyes that seemed to look deep into the past. "His name doesn't matter." Grandmother glanced at Lizzie. "The point is, Lizzie, you can't let the past hold you hostage. You need to move on and find someone, so you don't make the same mistakes. That boy you were crazy about in college is water under the bridge. Don't let him keep you from finding someone who will truly make you happy." Grandma patted her arm. "My mother spent a long time alone. It took her nearly seventeen years before she married my father. He was a widower with two young sons."

Lizzie's throat tightened. Had she let her bad experience with Geoff in college make her critical toward men? She nodded in agreement, unable to produce audible words.

Lizzie sat numbly, listening to her grandmother as she reminisced and shared the stories concerning the Crazy Quilt and events at the 1904 World's Fair. She forced herself to ask questions so that she wouldn't appear to be totally ignoring her grandmother. She really did want to listen intently to the tale, but inner turmoil raged a war with her consciousness.

After Grandma Mullane finished her story, Lizzie folded the quilt. "I'll put it away for you."

Grandma clasped Lizzie's hand. Soft, frail fingers gripped her gently. "No, dear." Grandma patted Lizzie's hand before placing her own hand back in her lap. "I want you to keep it—it's yours now."

"Oh, Grandma." Lizzie clutched the quilt to her chest. "Are you sure?"

Grandma Mullane nodded. "It's time it was passed down."

"Thank you."

Lizzie knew she needed to move on and let go of the pain she still harbored from Geoff's betrayal. She felt a lot like her great-great-grandmother, Elizabeth. She didn't want to settle for anything less than true love.

When Lizzie laid down in her grandmother's spare bedroom, her mind whirled with thoughts of the past, back to the time of her great-great-grandmother in 1904. Lizzie's own heartache after Geoff's betrayal was so heart-wrenching, she could sympathize with Elizabeth's broken heart, and how she'd left behind a quilt that not only told her story but held many secrets. Lizzie wrapped herself in the Crazy Quilt and fell asleep.

Chapter Two

"Come on, Elizabeth. Wake up!"

"Leave me alone." Lizzie pushed at the hand shaking her. She blinked several times and lifted to her elbows.

Two young girls stared at her, smiles beaming from ear to ear.

Lizzie glanced from the taller of the two, a girl with curly blonde hair and freckles sprinkled across the bridge of her nose, to the smaller girl who was a curly brunette with a cute button nose. She wore a beautiful pink dress with puffy sleeves, a weird collar with ruffles, and the tie for the dress was at hip level instead of around the waist or underneath the chest. The older girl's cream-colored dress had a lace collar and was equally outdated, yet they both appeared to be in brand new condition. Lizzie frowned. They looked harmless enough. "What in the world is going on? Who are you?"

The smaller of the two girls covered her mouth, turned to the other girl, and giggled. "Sissy is being silly."

The other put her hands on her hips and stared smugly at Lizzie. "If you think you're going to get us, you're not."

"Get you?" Lizzie frowned. "What are you talking about?"

"It's All Fool's Day." The older girl crossed her arms in front of her. "You already promised us yesterday that you would take us to see the progress at the World's Fair. So, it can't be a joke. You have to take us."

"Yeah." The younger of the two also crossed her arms defiantly. "You have to take us. No pulling pranks on us, Sissy, or I'm going to tell Daddy."

Their expressions would be funny—if Lizzie knew who they were and what was going on. "I'm sorry, girls. Honestly, I don't know who either of you are. And why do you keep referring to me as Sissy?"

"Because you're our big sister." The smaller munchkin put her hands to her hips. "Now stop playing, Elizabeth."

"Lizzie, please. Call me Lizzie." She didn't have any sisters, though she always wanted them. Instead, she had two older brothers. Lizzie stretched, hoping it would clear her foggy head. As she sat up in bed, the white, eyelet comforter slid down. "Where's the quilt?" She grasped the cover and tossed it back, looking for the quilt her great-grandmother had given her the night before. It wasn't here. Her heart beat so hard it pounded in her ears.

"Your fabric is in the chair, silly." The older girl pointed to a chair in the corner of the room. "Now, get ready so we can go. You can start working on the quilt you wanted to make tonight after we get back home." She grabbed the younger girl by the arm. "Come on, Olivia. Let's go finish setting the table for breakfast while Elizabeth—" She paused and glanced over her shoulder toward her. "I mean Lizzie, gets ready."

Lizzie resisted the urge to flop back against her pillow. Either this was an elaborate April Fool's prank, or she was having the most vivid dream she'd ever had! Great-grandma Mullane had just mentioned the World's Fair to her last night—so this had to be a dream. She tried to recall what she'd eaten for dinner the night before. "Normally oriental food makes me have weird dreams, but I haven't had any since Wednesday," Lizzie muttered to herself as she made her way to the mirror.

She clasped her arms around herself. "Where are my clothes?" she hollered, as she stared at her reflection in the mirror. This wasn't funny! When she went to bed last night, she had on pajama pants. The thought of someone having changed her into this old-fashioned, cotton nightgown with lace and pink trim made her cheeks grow warm.

Lizzie ran to the window and looked outside. She was on the second story of a home, surrounded by other homes, much larger than that of her grandmothers'. The few vehicles parked on the road were not modern. They resembled the old-fashioned collectors' cars she'd seen at the car shows.

She stormed out of the bedroom she'd woken up in and headed down the stairs toward the sound of voices. In the dining room, she found the two little girls seated at the table. A man wearing a suit sat at one end, and at the other end sat a woman whose dress looked as if it came right out of the movie, *Meet Me in St. Louis*. Presumably, these were her captors, although a very odd sort.

Lizzie planted a fist firmly on each hip. "I demand to know what is going on."

The man carefully folded his newspaper and laid it aside on the table. "Elizabeth Ruth Ambrewster, don't you think it was time you stopped teasing your sisters?"

"My sisters? I don't have any sisters. And how do you know my name?" She blinked rapidly as dawning set in. "My last name is Peterson, not Ambrewster. That was my great-great-grandmother's maiden name."

The couple frowned as they stared at her.

13

Lizzie glanced toward the children to see how they reacted to her revelation. Olivia, as the other girl had called her, eyes glistened as they began to well up with tears.

She might as well have told the poor child Santa Claus wasn't real. "I'm sorry," Lizzie said. "I've always wanted a sister, but right now, I feel like someone is playing an elaborate April Fool's joke on me."

"Now, dear, what makes you think such a thing?" the woman at the other end of the table asked. Her expression turned serious as she glanced back toward the man. "You don't think she has hit her head and can't remember things, do you?"

Lizzie bit her lower lip to keep from laughing at how ludicrous it all sounded. She hadn't hit her head. "You never answered me." She mustered up the courage to sound demanding, "How do you know my name and how did I get here?"

"Enough of this nonsense, Elizabeth. You're our daughter, so obviously we know your name." Frown lines creased the man's forehead. "If you continue behaving this way then… then… I'll seriously consider having you locked up for being crazy."

The woman gasped. "John, you wouldn't?!"

His left eyebrow arched. "Well, Rose, if our daughter insists on acting like we are all a bunch of strangers, or worse yet, criminals, then I have no choice."

"I'm not crazy," Lizzie protested. What should she do? She didn't want to be locked up. Thus far, these people had been hospitable. They acted like they knew her and didn't appear to be joking—unfortunately—about incarcerating her either.

Lizzie tried to think of a reason for why this was all happening. If these people had kidnapped her, they had gone to elaborate lengths to do so. Her family wasn't rich, so it didn't make sense that anyone would go as far as to rent old-time vehicles.

Weird food made her dream. Maybe she was hallucinating? She didn't feel like she was drugged. The room wasn't swaying. Lizzie pinched her arm. Ouch. That hurt. The only explanation left was she had to be dreaming. Was it possible to feel pain while you were dreaming?

But what would cause her to have such an obscure dream? Especially if she hadn't eaten Chinese or anything she could recall that would make her have weird dreams.

Was this how Dorothy felt in the Wizard of Oz? As long as she didn't come across any witches, good or bad, she'd let this silly dream play out, and in the morning, she'd wake up in the same bed that she went to sleep in last night—wrapped in her great-great-grandmother's quilt.

Chapter Three

As Lizzie glanced in the mirror, she smoothed her hands over the fabric of the pink dress with white lace and frill on top, thankful she had a slender waist, considering the puffy bottom of the dress made her hips look wider. The dress was one of the many elaborate ones she'd found in her great-great-grandmother's armoire. She'd also discovered numerous hat boxes, yet she refused to don such an item. She felt ridiculous enough as it was. "Good thing this is only a dream," she told herself. "I'd never be caught out in public like this."

At least the little calf boots she wore were cute, something she'd consider buying in the future—whenever she woke up from this dream.

Lizzie retraced her steps to the dining room. The table had been cleared of all the dishes, except one, with some cut-up fruit, scrambled eggs, and bacon. Presumably, a plate left for her—she hoped.

"You look lovely in that dress. It has always been one of my favorites," the woman who was at the table earlier said as she came into the room. "I trust that you're feeling better?"

"Yes." She didn't want to disagree with the woman or suggest that perhaps the woman and her entire family might be better candidates for the *funny farm* than she was. "I'm afraid I didn't ask you earlier. What should I call you?"

"Call me?" The woman's left eyebrow arched momentarily before she squinted and rushed toward her, placing the back of her hand against Lizzie's forehead. "Oh, dear. You're not running a fever." She ushered her to the table and pulled out a chair for her to sit down. "You haven't hit your head, have you?"

Lizzie shook her head, touched by the compassion the woman displayed.

"Perhaps I should call your father back home." She knelt by Lizzie's side. "He left for work a few moments ago."

"My father?"

"Yes, dear, and I'm your mother." She gently patted her hand.

Well, that answered two questions. She still had another. "What city do we live in?"

The woman known as Mother blinked a couple times, then stood, placing a hand firmly on each hip. "Elizabeth Ruth, how dare you play such an ugly April Fool's joke on your mother. I was frantically worried about you!"

Lizzie forced a laugh. "I'm sorry. I didn't mean to frighten you." If this whole situation hadn't been incredulous and only a dream, albeit the weirdest and most vivid dream she'd ever had, she would have been frightened herself.

Mother's features softened as a smile crept upon her lips. "I'm afraid your breakfast has gotten cold."

"It's all right." Lizzie smiled in return. "I'll just pop it into the microwave and it'll be fine."

"Seriously, Elizabeth. Are you going to be like this all day?" Mother sighed. "And pray tell, what is a microwave? Another obscure thing from that vivid imagination of yours?"

"Uh…" The woman didn't know what a microwave was? Maybe she was playing a prank on Lizzie now? Then Lizzie remembered the old-fashioned cars she'd spotted when she looked out the bedroom window earlier. What could she say? If she wasn't careful, dream or no dream, these people would surely have her committed. Now, even she doubted her own sanity.

"Aren't you done eating yet, Elizabeth?" The oldest of the two little girls claiming to be her sister placed her hands on her hips—obviously a trait passed down in this family. "You know we have to hurry if we want to catch the train."

"Mary Margaret, go get Olivia and make sure you've both washed up before you go." Mother placed the plate of food in front of Elizabeth and handed her the fork. "I'll see to it that your sister eats, and you'll be on your way in no time."

"Thank you." Elizabeth took the fork and ate, telling herself it wasn't any different than eating cold pizza, which tasted better than cold eggs and bacon. At least the fruit tasted refreshing.

Fifteen minutes later, she was heading out the door with Olivia and Mary Margaret both tugging on her arms.

"If you're not going to wear a hat, at least make sure to take your parasol and don't forget your coin purse. I've already put the money your father gave me for your adventure today in it," Mother said, extending a white frilly umbrella to Lizzie and handing her a small white coin purse. Then Mother leaned toward Lizzie and kissed her on the cheek before kissing both younger girls.

Lizzie blushed. When was the last time her own mother had kissed her? This woman was endearing; and apparently, she wasn't a prisoner if she could take her two young charges out for the day.

"Make sure to mind your sister today," Mother said, and held the door open while the girls left.

Once they got to the bottom of the stairs, Lizzie didn't know which way to go. What she wouldn't give for her cell phone with the GPS. She started to turn toward the right, but both girls tugged at her arms. "This way, Elizabeth."

She couldn't help but laugh. It reminded her of a small child trying to pull a dog on a leash—only this time, she was the dog and she had no idea which way to go. In a sense, she felt as disoriented as a dog, not sure where to go from here. She could drag the girls along anywhere she really wanted to go, but she'd only get them lost. "Why don't we make a game of our adventure. Since both of you know the way so well, why don't you lead me?"

"Yeah," they squealed in delight.

"I love games," Olivia announced.

Lizzie smiled at Olivia's enthusiasm, but doubted her ability to lead them to the train station. "How old are you, Olivia?"

She held up her left hand, all her fingers spread wide. "I'm five."

"And since I'm eight and the oldest, I get to lead the way." Mary Margaret tugged on her arm. "We need to go this way."

They started to cross the street, but Olivia planted her feet firmly and tugged. "No! I want to go this way."

Mary Margaret stopped, turned around and moved in front of Olivia, never letting go of Lizzie's arm. "We're not going to the candy store. If you keep stopping, we are going to miss the train."

As if echoing in agreement, a train whistle sounded in the near distance.

"On, no," Mary Margaret exclaimed.

"We'll get candy later, Olivia." Lizzie turned the girls toward the direction Mary Margaret had been heading a moment earlier. "We better hurry. Lead the way."

Lizzie scampered toward the sound of the train. Mary Margaret picked up on the urgency and took off at a brisk pace as poor Olivia struggled to keep up, hindered by her tiny legs. She scooped Olivia up in her arms and quickly hurried to follow her sister. How she wished she was wearing a pair of sweat pants and tennis shoes right now!

Chapter Four

"I need three tickets for..." Where were they going? Lizzie panted, exhausted from carrying Olivia at a brisk pace for three blocks to make it to the train station on time.

"We're going to the World's Fair," Olivia added.

"Thank you, Olivia." Lizzie smiled and gently set her young charge down. She opened her coin purse, thumbed through the dollar bills and change, and briskly closed the purse when she realized there wasn't enough money inside to pay for their tickets. Her cheeks felt warm. It normally cost her a minimum of forty dollars one way, if she was lucky enough to buy a discount ticket to St. Louis. "I'm sorry, girls. I only have around seventy dollars."

"Shh—," the ticket salesman whispered. "You don't want to let anyone know you are carrying a lot of money. A pretty girl like you might get robbed."

"You think I'm pretty?" Lizzie blushed. That wasn't the point of the conversation, even though it was flattering. She stepped closer to the counter and lowered her voice. "Seventy dollars isn't very much money, surely not enough to buy three tickets to St. Louis and back, not to mention something to eat while we are there."

The man laughed. "Missy, that'll be plenty of money. It only costs ten dollars for a round-trip train ticket to St. Louis."

"That's it?" her voice squeaked.

"Yes, ma'am," the kindly, aging man told her.

23

Lizzie took thirty dollars out of the coin purse and paid him. It would take a while for her mind to readjust to thinking back to 1904, the only time the World's Fair had been in St. Louis. Why her mind decided to dream of such a period she had no idea, other than her grandmother mentioning it the night before. She'd never been partial to history. Perhaps the World's Fair held the answer to her getting back home?

After the man gave Lizzie the tickets, she took hold of each of the girls' hand and headed for the train platform. Even for that time period, seventy dollars sounded like a lot of money to give your oldest daughter for a day's outing. "What does our father do for a living again?"

"He's a banker, silly," Mary Margaret announced nonchalantly. "You're not trying to tease us again are you, Sissy?"

Lizzie shook her head. A father with money? Too bad that wasn't a reality! Her real father was a carpenter. It was a good trade, and she admired his ability to take a blueprint and turn it into a home or business. "We'd best hurry and catch the train. They're boarding now."

Mary Margaret climbed the steps to board the train. Placing a hand firmly beneath each arm, Lizzie hoisted Olivia up the first stair before grabbing hold of her long dress to raise it slightly so that she could follow. Her dress caught on something, and she stumbled backwards.

Firm hands grasped her, holding her tight against something solid. She glanced over her shoulder and locked gazes with the bluest eyes, the type she'd only seen a German Shepherd have. She was hypnotized by them, and the smell of his aftershave.

His lips moved, but she didn't comprehend what he said.

"Excuse me?" she mumbled.

He smiled, revealing perfectly straight teeth. Definitely a dream. Guys that looked this good in reality had other flaws. She took a moment to focus her attention on the rest of his face but straightened when she realized how young he looked. "You're not very old."

His chuckle made her blush. "I'll be twenty-three on the fourth of July."

"Hmm..." Substantially younger than she was. Figured, even dreams couldn't be perfect.

"How old are you?" he asked.

"I'm twenty-eight."

"She is not," Mary Margaret said, standing with her hands on her hips. "She keeps playing jokes on people because today is All Fool's Day. She's only twenty-one."

"I am not..." Lizzie thought back to her reflection in the mirror that morning. She'd been more concerned with where she was, she hadn't paid as much attention to her features, other than the fact that the image staring back at her was herself.

"So," he said. "You're not playing a joke, or you're not twenty-one?"

Lizzie straightened, hoisted her dress slightly, and spoke over her shoulder as she continued up the stairs, "Don't you know it's not polite to ask a lady her age?"

She found seats together near a window for her and the girls, having the youngest sit next to her, and Mary Margaret across from them so that she could look out the window, too.

As the train pulled out of the station, Lizzie thought about how transportation had changed over the years. The train was an older model than she was accustomed to, like one out of the pictures she'd seen at the train museum.

Modern technology was wonderful. They'd improved on the design in later years, including how smoothly trains glided across railroad tracks.

Trading coal for diesel improved the smell at a train station. Although, it was kind of nice that you had the ability to open the windows on the older trains. It felt odd to think of the train as older, given it looked to be in pristine condition.

"Tickets, please."

Lizzie startled, grabbed the tickets from her lap to hand them to the porter, and paused with her hand in the air, mouth gaping. "It's you."

He chuckled and gently touched his index finger to her chin, applying a little pressure as he raised her chin. "You might catch flies if you're not careful."

Both the girls giggled.

Lizzie turned and frowned at them, which quieted them, although Olivia was only silenced by placing her own hand over her mouth to suppress her laughter.

"By the way," the young man said. "I didn't get the chance to introduce myself earlier. My name is Jeremiah Hopkins. And what might be the names of you lovely ladies?"

Mary Margaret told him her name, and Olivia quickly uncovered her mouth and blurted out her name before returning her hand to her mouth.

"And our big sister's name is—"

"None of his business, Mary Margaret." Lizzie forced a brief smile and handed Jeremiah their tickets. "It's really not good for the children to talk to strangers."

"I'm sorry, Elizabeth," Mary Margaret said.

"That's a beautiful name." Jeremiah handed her back the portion of the ticket they would need for their return trip. "For a beautiful woman."

"Thank you." Lizzie rolled her eyes and placed their return stubs in her lap. Surely, he could come up with a better pick-up line than that?

"I will see you later, ladies." Jeremiah tipped his hat and continued with his job.

"He likes you," Mary Margaret announced.

Olivia giggled and shook her head in agreement.

"You can take your hand off your mouth now, Olivia." Lizzie sighed. "And it doesn't matter if he likes me. This is only a dream, and in the morning, I'll wake up and won't be here."

Olivia gasped. "No!"

"What do you mean?" Mary Margaret exclaimed. "You're not leaving, are you? If you're playing a joke again, Daddy's going to be angry."

"Calm down, girls." Wasn't this the part in the dream where you were supposed to wake up? It hadn't happened yet. "Look, right now, we're all dreaming, and this is a fun and adventurous dream. Let's enjoy it while we can."

"But I don't want you to leave, Sissy." Tears welled up in Olivia's eyes.

Lizzie had to go, she needed to get back to her time and her family. She could only do that if she woke up. But until then, no sense in having a frantic night's sleep. "Don't worry girls. I'll still be here tomorrow." Not the *here* they had in mind, but alive and kicking, and if Jeremiah Hopkins made any more comments about her catching flies with her mouth open, she was likely to do some kicking in her sleep as well!

Chapter Five

While Lizzie had always wanted a sister, she hadn't envisioned having two, especially sisters who were so much younger than herself. Their train ride to St. Louis was nearly over, and she dreaded the return trip. It had been interesting to see how the city used to look.

Hopefully, the girls would be tired by the time they finished doing some sightseeing and would settle down on the way home. Lizzie smiled to herself. Funny how her dream began to feel real enough to start referring to the place where she woke up this morning as her home.

"You should smile more often."

"Is that so?" Lizzie asked, recognizing Jeremiah's voice without having to look up at him. He'd made a point of talking to all the other passengers around them, waving or smiling at the girls when they would giggle or smile at him, and managing to ignore her for the last three hours. Not that she needed him for anything.

"Quite so." Jeremiah smiled, and as much as Lizzie tried, she couldn't refrain the smile that crept across her face. "And I was thinking, since I have a couple hours layover until I must work on the return trip home, I thought perhaps you lovely ladies would help me to occupy my time by having lunch with me. Then I could give you a tour of the World's Fair before it opens."

She never would have envisioned herself dreaming of men dressed in suits or dress pants, riding the train to and from work. Or women in long, fancy dresses for everyday wear. Jeremiah's jacket was the only thing that seemed different for a conductor, compared to her time period.

"I don't know…" Lizzie frowned. Jeremiah seemed charming enough, but that didn't mean he was trustworthy. Of course, if this were a nightmare, the dream would have already turned bad.

"I understand." Jeremiah nodded politely and turned to go.

"Stop—" Lizzie's cheeks warmed. "Sorry. I didn't mean to yell."

Jeremiah turned and came back, pausing to lean on the seat in front of her. He grinned.

"We would be happy to join you," Lizzie said.

The girls both cheered.

She told herself the reason she agreed to accompany him was for the girls' sake. Not to mention, his guidance and directions would be beneficial. Lizzie had no idea where she was going. So far, the only thing recognizable on the way to St. Louis had been the endless cow pastures. Not that homes had changed a tremendous amount over the years, the usual landmarks she'd grown accustomed to when traveling back and forth to her parents and grandparents along the way from Warrensburg to St. Louis were different from modern day. The absence of chain restaurants disoriented her. Normally, she knew where she'd see the familiar golden arches or other familiar electronic signs.

"After I've helped the passengers who will be exiting the train, I will meet you three lovely ladies on the platform." Jeremiah tipped his hat, turned, and headed back up the aisle.

Lizzie smiled as he walked away, wondering what he looked like in street clothes. His dark blue jacket was longer, somewhat like a sports jacket, which kept her from getting the *view* she preferred. His shoulders looked broad and tapered to a slender waistline. His wavy hair was sure to have a crease in it from his hat. Geoff's used to from…his baseball cap. Lizzie swallowed the lump in her throat. Her ex-boyfriend was another bad dream she didn't want to relive.

The scent of cherry drew her attention. It smelled pleasant. The guy in the seat behind them must have lit his pipe again. You didn't see people do that now-a-days… or in her time period. Amtrak didn't allow smoking on trains. She wondered how people in this century would feel if they had a chance to glimpse into the future. Men and women in shorts, showing more bare legs, would probably make the people on this train gasp. Lizzie chuckled to herself.

"Are we almost there?" Olivia yawned and stretched. "I'm hungry."

"Almost, sweetie." Lizzie brushed a few stray strands of hair from the little girl's face and smiled. As if echoing in response, the train whistle blared, and the train began to slow. She clutched her tickets in her hand and picked up her parasol that had fallen to the floor during their ride. "When we get up to exit the train, I need both of you girls to take hold of my hand so that we don't get separated."

Mary Margaret nodded. Olivia stood, anxious to get up and move after being confined for nearly four hours. Once the train came to a complete stop, Lizzie stood to make sure the girls obeyed and didn't rush past her.

"Go ahead, ladies." The middle-aged man with the pipe in the seat behind them motioned for them to exit before him. People were more formal and polite than she was accustomed to.

"Thank you." Lizzie took a hand of each girl, wishing she could hold on tighter. She transferred the closed parasol to her other hand, with the tickets and coin purse, and clutched Olivia's hand firmer. The youngest girl tended to be the more restless of the two.

Once they exited the train, Lizzie ushered the girls to a bench on the platform. "Let's sit down and wait for Jeremiah."

"I don't want to sit." Olivia stomped her foot and stood firm.

Lizzie tried to pull on her arm, but she refused to budge.

"No."

"No?" Lizzie laughed. Okay, being obstinate also fit her youngest sister's character traits. Perhaps having a baby sister left room to be desired. "How about this, I'll sit on the bench and you and Mary Margaret can skip in a circle in front of me until Jeremiah comes?"

That prospect apparently worked because Olivia's eyes sparkled as a smile crept upon her face, and she began skipping. This time, she practically pulled Lizzie in her haste to reach the bench. Mary Margaret quickly joined in. Lizzie giggled like a school girl and started skipping, too. After all, it was only a dream. She didn't have to worry about anyone seeing her that she knew from her past. Why not have fun?

"All right, girls. We're here. I'll sit down while the two of you skip back and forth." Thankfully, they willingly released her hands. Lizzie sat her things on the bench and pulled her skirt up slightly in order to tuck a leg beneath her when she sat down.

The crowd of people who'd exited the train, along with the new passengers who'd boarded the train, thinned. Lizzie wondered if Jeremiah had forgotten about his promise, or them. Then she saw him hanging on the railing as he climbed down the stairs, pausing to say something to a coworker. The other guy looked toward them and waved. Her cheeks warmed. She wondered what Jeremiah told his friend. Obviously that he had someone waiting for him.

Lizzie pretended to be preoccupied with watching the girls as Jeremiah approached. He had unbuttoned his jacket and had his hands tucked in his pockets.

"The girls look like they are having fun," Jeremiah said as he took a seat next to Lizzie on the bench.

She nodded. "It was hard for them being cooped up on the train for four hours. They needed to let off a little nervous energy."

"It seems like their older sister needed to let off energy, too." Jeremiah sat back and put his arm behind Lizzie and smiled. "I noticed you skipped as well."

Her cheeks warmed. "You weren't supposed to see that." She giggled.

Jeremiah reached up and twirled one of Lizzie's curls. "I think it was cute. Your sisters absolutely adore you."

Lizzie didn't want to correct him, after all, this was only a dream. "Perhaps we should be going now. I'm sure both of the girls are hungry."

Jeremiah stood and took her hand, helping her up. He continued to hold her hand. "Come on, girls," he said. "Let's all hold hands together."

How could she refute his request, when the girls gleefully joined in and grabbed each of their hands? "What should I do with my umbrella?"

Jeremiah paused, then looked at the parasol on the bench. He retrieved the umbrella for Lizzie, opened it, and handed it to her.

"Thank you."

He gently took her arm at the elbow and clasped Olivia's hand again. "Now we're ready to go." He winked at Lizzie.

With Jeremiah around, she wouldn't need to wear blush. Her cheeks always felt warm, and not from the sun. Why didn't modern day men possess such charm?

Chapter Six

Once they reached the fairgrounds, Lizzie could not believe the huge expanse of exhibits, and wondered if they would be able to see everything. The area looked quite different from what it was in modern times.

Jeremiah continued to hold both her and Olivia's hands as he led them past several interesting exhibits still under construction that Lizzie would have liked to visit. "You will love my aunt's cooking," Jeremiah said. "She and my Uncle Frank have a quaint restaurant at the fair."

Lizzie smiled, hoping they would reach the restaurant soon.

"Are we there yet?" Olivia asked. "I'm hungry."

Almost as if in response, Lizzie's stomach growled.

Jeremiah laughed. "We will be there shortly." He nodded up the road. "See the restaurant with the canopy?"

Mary Margaret nodded and said, "yes."

"That is where we are headed." Jeremiah increased his pace, forcing the girls to hurry their steps.

"I'm tired of walking," Olivia announced, and Lizzie almost laughed. On the train, Olivia couldn't wait to get up and move around, and now she wanted to sit down.

Without letting go of Lizzie's hand, Jeremiah paused long enough to scoop Olivia up in his arm. She giggled and flung her arms around his neck. "You'll be sitting and eating in no time, my lady."

"Good. I'm hungry." Olivia glanced past Jeremiah to look at Lizzie. "She's hungry, too. Did you hear her tummy growl?"

Lizzie blushed. "I think you're a bit too outspoken."

Jeremiah's laugh was hearty. "I think you've gone and embarrassed your sister."

"She's not—" Lizzie caught herself. She'd have the girls in tears if she mentioned not being their sister. Even if this was a dream, she didn't want to see either of them cry.

"Then by all means, continue being honest," Jeremiah said. "Apparently, your sister isn't embarrassed. The early afternoon sun is merely turning her cheeks rosy."

"You're even more impossible than she is." Lizzie pulled her hand from his.

"I'm sorry." His expression sobered. "I was only having fun."

"Apparently at my expense," Lizzie mumbled.

"Jeremiah!" a well-rounded, middle-aged woman called out before they reached the tables and chairs on the sidewalk outside the restaurant. "How good to see you."

Jeremiah hugged the woman. "Aunt JoAnn, this is Olivia."

"I'm very pleased to meet you, young miss." Aunt JoAnn gently tapped the end of Olivia's nose with her index finger, and Olivia giggled. "And who might these other two lovely ladies be?"

"My name is Lizzie, and this is… my younger sister, Mary Margaret." Lizzie extended her hand, but JoAnn just glanced at it a moment.

"Isn't that something men folk do?" She looked at Lizzie, stepped closer and hugged her. "It's nice to meet you, dear."

"She hugs everybody," Jeremiah said. "We thought we'd stop for lunch and do some sightseeing."

"Wonderful." JoAnn pulled out a chair at one of the tables. "It's nice outside today. Why don't you all have a seat out here?"

Jeremiah sat Olivia in the seat next to the one his aunt had pulled out.

Mary Margaret took the seat offered. "Thank you."

"I just pulled a batch of fried chicken out of the fryer," JoAnn said. "I will bring you all some of it, along with the fixings."

Lizzie smiled because she didn't know what to do. Once Jeremiah's aunt was out of earshot, she turned to him. "I take it we don't get to look at a menu to order?"

He chuckled. "My aunt is old-fashioned."

Lizzie frowned. *As opposed to what?* She wondered. After all, they were living in ancient times.

"She likes to keep people fed." Jeremiah scooted his chair closer to the table and leaned closer to Lizzie. "Technically, they're not opened until the fair opens. So, she and my uncle cook to feed the many workers."

"Ah." Lizzie nodded. It explained why the fairgrounds weren't crowded. She hadn't noticed any other people wandering around like they were, taking in the sights. They had seen a boy playing ball with a dog, but one of the construction workers had called out to him by name. She assumed he'd brought his son to work with him. Her stomach grumbled again. She didn't fancy chicken on a bone. "Any chance they'd have chicken fingers?"

"Eww," the girls complained.

Jeremiah laughed so hard his chest shook.

"What?" She stared at Jeremiah, noting how cute his dimples were when he cut loose with laughter.

He wiped the moisture from his eyes. "You do realize chickens don't have fingers, don't you?"

Lizzie nodded. "Yeah." She thought for a moment. "Oh, you mean when I asked about chicken fingers?"

Jeremiah nodded. "Yes, they have claws."

"You're right." She couldn't help but giggle. "Where I come from, chicken fingers are boneless, skinless, breaded and fried pieces of chicken breast. Very delicious."

"And where might you come from?" Jeremiah's expression sobered. "I overheard your sisters complaining earlier about you playing pranks on them. This wouldn't be one of those pranks you're trying to play on me is it?"

A lump formed in her throat. She nodded.

"It is All Fool's Day, after all." Jeremiah leaned toward her again, reaching to tuck a strand of hair behind her ear. "Something tells me you like to have fun."

Even though the way Jeremiah said it didn't sound suggestive, like most guys she knew would insinuate, she still blushed.

Thankfully, his aunt showed up, with presumably a helper, carrying four plates of food. "Here you go."

They set the beautiful plates, that were designed with an image of Thomas Jefferson, surrounded by five images of palaces at the fair and another of a garden, in front of them. The two girls received smaller portions and a glass of lemonade, while hot tea was placed in front of Jeremiah and Lizzie. "Do you think I could trouble you for some ice?" Lizzie asked.

"Sure, dear." JoAnn instructed the male server to retrieve her request. "If you all need anything else, just let me know." JoAnn winked at Jeremiah and went back inside.

Lizzie had the sneaking suspicion Aunt JoAnn was doing the math, and she'd added it up all wrong. She and Jeremiah were not an item. Not that he wasn't cute, in a boyish sort of way. But he was nearly five years younger than she was, at least her real age. Apparently, all one needed to do to become younger was get their beauty rest. It'd already taken seven years off of her.

She picked at her chicken in silence. It really was delicious, even though it had bones. A couple moments later, their server brought her a bowl with an ice cube. Did he think she was a dog and wanted to drink out of a bowl?

"Excuse me," she said, before he walked away. "Could you bring me a glass of ice?"

"I would be happy to." He nodded and left.

"I'm not even going to ask." Jeremiah smiled and took another bite of his chicken.

Lizzie stirred a couple of teaspoons of sugar into her tea, noting the man quizzically watching her from the table next to theirs. When their server returned with her glass of ice, she poured the cup of tea into it and took a sip. "Ah, now that's refreshing. Nothing like a nice cold glass of iced tea."

The man at the other table smirked. "Waiter, may I have one of those?"

"Yes, Mr. Blechynden," the waiter replied. "Would you like me to put it together like the lady did as well?"

"No, I'd like to do it myself. Thank you." He motioned the waiter away and addressed Lizzie, "What did you say that drink was called?"

"Iced tea." Lizzie giggled. "Haven't you ever had it before?"

The man shook his head.

Lizzie took another sip and paused. Weren't there some timeline continuum rules or something? Good thing this was only a dream, or she may be altering the future.

Chapter Seven

"I can't wait for the fair to open," Lizzie said. "It will be even more exciting than it has been today." Three hours of wandering around the fairgrounds made the girls and her tired. They were heading back to the entrance, so they could catch the train back home.

"Look at the puppies." Olivia pointed to three dogs tied up near a group of Filipino men.

None of the men wore shirts, not something Lizzie expected in this era. She noticed their muscular build, which they had obviously acquired without a gym membership.

"Perhaps we should walk another way," Jeremiah suggested, and began to lead them away from the men. His pursed lips and narrowed eyes made Lizzie wonder why he disapproved of the men.

"Oh please, Sissy, can't we go pet the dogs?" Mary Margaret asked.

Olivia didn't wait for a response. She pulled free of Jeremiah's hold and ran to pet one of the stray mutts. All three dogs began to lick her and jump on her.

The men laughed. Lizzie could not tell what they were saying in their language. She assumed they enjoyed seeing the dogs' reaction to Olivia. Mary Margaret and Lizzie both squatted down to pet a dog as well, leaving Olivia the smallest of the three dogs to pet.

"Don't you want to pet one, Jeremiah?" Lizzie smiled up at him.

Jeremiah stood with his hands tucked in his pockets. His gaze remained on the men watching them. "No, thank you," he said. "I think we should be leaving now or we will miss the train."

Lizzie nodded and stood. "Come on girls, Jeremiah's right. We need to get a move on if we want to catch the train on time."

The girls both reluctantly hugged a dog and pet all three one last time before they turned to leave, looking over their shoulders at the dogs while they walked away.

"I wish Daddy would let us have a dog," Olivia said. "Maybe for my birthday."

This wasn't a conversation Lizzie wanted to have. If their parents didn't want them to have a dog, who was she to encourage it?

Lizzie allowed the girls to walk slightly ahead of them so that she could talk to Jeremiah. "Is there a reason you didn't like those Filipino men?"

"If you ask me, they should be wearing clothing."

"They had clothing on." Lizzie giggled. "Does it bother you to see other men shirtless?"

"I would think it would bother you." Jeremiah's tone was curt.

Her smile slowly faded. She constantly had to remind herself that this place was ancient. Jeremiah would be shocked if he rode the subway or visited any large city and saw how people dressed or listened to the way they talked. "Seeing someone shirtless doesn't bother me. I felt like there was more to it, like something else was bothering you."

Jeremiah shrugged.

"Why wouldn't you pet the dogs?" Lizzie asked.

"Because I know the fate the Filipino tribe of Igorot have planned for the dogs." His lips pursed again. "It is their custom to eat dogs."

Lizzie gasped, covering her mouth with her hand. "You've got to be kidding?"

Jeremiah nodded. "No. It is part of their diet and it has been allowed since they are visiting our country and sharing their culture as part of the World's Fair attraction."

"Surely we could get people to protest?" Even though this was part of a dream, Lizzie felt sick to her stomach. "It's barbaric, if you ask me."

"I agree." Jeremiah placed a comforting arm around her as they walked.

It was nice having Jeremiah with them on the trip today. Lizzie was thankful he was there to help them get back to the train station and board the proper train. She smiled at the thought of getting to spend another four hours with him on the ride back home.

Shortly after they were all seated, the girls both leaned against the window and began to doze. They'd had a fun and exhausting day. When Jeremiah got to them, Lizzie held out her tickets, but did not readily release them when he grabbed them. "Are you sure you couldn't sit with us for a little while?"

Jeremiah smiled. "You know that I would like nothing more."

"Jeremiah, is that you?" A beautiful blonde with her hair done up fancy walked up to Jeremiah, laid a delicate hand against his chest and kissed him on the cheek. "It's good to see you again. My mother is hoping you will come by for supper again soon."

The hurt and pain Geoff caused Lizzie came flooding back. Jeremiah wasn't her boyfriend, and she would do well to remember that.

The woman turned to Lizzie. "Hello. My name is Rose Marie Russell." She glanced at Jeremiah, batted her eyelashes, and squeezed her arms around his bicep. "Jeremiah says I'm his favorite flower."

"Perhaps you should return to your seat?" Jeremiah gently removed the woman's hands. "If you ladies will excuse me, I should get back to work." He tipped his cap and walked away.

He's not your boyfriend, Lizzie reminded herself. *And he's never going to be! Player!*

"May I join you?" Rose asked, motioning to the seat next to Mary Margaret.

"Actually—" Lizzie propped her feet on the seat. "The girls and I are rather tired. I think I'm going to close my eyes for a bit while they are napping." Lizzie leaned her head back, crossed her arms and closed her eyes, forcing herself not to smile at the intentional snub.

The *hmph,* as Rose walked away did Lizzie's resolve in, as a smile creased her lips. Served Blondie right.

An hour later, Lizzie moved her head back and forth, trying to pop her aching neck. Her eyes slowly fluttered open.

"Hello, sleepy." Jeremiah was seated in the row next to her. "Looks like today wore all three of you out."

His lazy smile gave her the warm-fuzzies. Until she remembered Rose. Lizzie's stomach churned. She could almost feel the bile creeping up in her throat. "I imagine you're pretty worn out yourself, especially with having to keep track of all the women you meet on the train each day." Lizzie batted her eyes like Rose had done earlier, and smiled sweetly, even when nothing about her mood felt sweet.

"I can explain." Jeremiah turned toward her, his legs straddling the edge of the seat, partially blocking the aisle. "I met her the other day on the train and she invited me over to dinner. I assure you it meant nothing. She mistook my intentions."

"Your intentions?" Lizzie laughed. "I don't see how you could have mistaken hers! But that's neither here nor there. You're a free agent and can do as you please."

"Agent?" Jeremiah's brows creased. "I'm not an agent."

"It's an old saying." Lizzie shook her head. "Never mind. It just means, we had a wonderful day. Thank you for helping to show my sisters and me around."

"Does that mean you forgive me?" Jeremiah's left eyebrow raised slightly, his head tilted, intent to find out her answer.

"There's nothing to forgive." She forced another sweet smile, then sighed. "You're just a nice guy who enjoys the company of women to occupy his time during shifts." He was nice. Nothing he'd done had been mean-spirited and she had no reason to expect anything more from him than friendship.

Jeremiah reached over and took hold of her hand. "Do you think I might see you again?"

"Sure." Lizzie pulled it away. "The next time we take a train." She wanted to say, *in your dreams*, but thought of how ironic it was considering this was her dream—one wrought with mixed emotions.

Jeremiah's head slumped. He nodded and stood, tipping his cap before he walked away.

She felt slightly guilty for his dejected look but shrugged it off as Mary Margaret began to wake and stretched while letting out a yawn.

"Hello, sleepyhead." Lizzie gently shook Olivia. "I'm going to miss this when I go back home in the morning."

Chapter Eight

By the time they reached home, had a bite to eat, and shared stories of their day with the girls' parents, Olivia and Mary Margaret were ready to go to bed. "I want to sleep with Sissy." Olivia wrapped her arms around Lizzie's neck. "She said she wouldn't be here tomorrow."

"I don't remember saying that." Lizzie saw the look of disapproval, she'd seen on her so-called mother's face this morning. "I'm not pulling pranks. I promise."

"You said it on the train when I woke up," Olivia reminded her.

Warmth filled her cheeks. Apparently, her youngest sister was more awake than she thought at the time.

"Can we both sleep with Sissy?" Mary Margaret folded her hands together, pleading with their mother.

"I think that would be a wonderful idea." Mother gave Lizzie a stern look. It must have been a look they taught at parenting school, because her own mother often gave her the same look, daring Lizzie to defy her.

"That's fine." Lizzie sighed. Hopefully, neither of the girls kicked people in their sleep. "Go brush your teeth and get your nightgowns on." Once the girls went running off to do as they were told, Lizzie stood to go. "I'll go get changed as well. Have a good night."

"Where are you going?" Mother asked.

Lizzie paused and looked at her. "I just said—"

Mother tapped her cheek with her index finger. "Don't tell me you think you are getting too old to kiss me good night?"

"Uh." What could she say? Lizzie walked over to the couch, bent and kissed Mother on the cheek. "Good night."

"Good night, dear."

Thankfully, their father had been occupied in the study or she may have been required to kiss him on the cheek as well. She didn't feel as comfortable with him, or Mother, as she did with the girls.

Lizzie barely finished changing into the gown she was wearing that morning when the girls burst into her room. At least Mary Margaret paused long enough to close the door. Then she ran and jumped on the bed to join Olivia, who was already getting nestled beneath the covers.

Situating herself in the middle of the girls, Lizzie reached over and turned off the Tiffany lamp on the nightstand.

"Aren't we going to pray?" Olivia asked.

Yawning kept Lizzie from letting out a sigh. "Sure, Olivia. Go ahead and pray."

Lizzie could tell by the moonlight shining through the window that both girls had clasped their hands in front of them. She couldn't help but smile, especially as Olivia prayed, making sure to ask God that her big sissy would be there in the morning.

Nice prayer, even if it wasn't about to come true. While it had been fun and relaxing not getting a gazillion text messages, she needed to get back to reality. Before she left for home tomorrow evening, she'd have to make her grandmothers lunch and have something ready for them for dinner as well. Just the thought of everything she had to do made her tired. Lizzie yawned and drifted off to sleep.

She dreamt of the World's Fair, the shirtless men who ate dogs, and of Jeremiah's aunt whom she'd suspected of trying to play matchmaker. The last dream was the most peaceful one of all.

In the morning, as the sun peeked through the slit of the curtains, Lizzie began to stretch and bumped something solid. An arm flopped across her. Her eyes popped open and she shot up to a sitting position. "Oh, no!" Lizzie blinked rapidly, as if it would change the view before her eyes. "It wasn't a dream!"

Chapter Nine

Olivia and Mary Margaret pounced on Lizzie with even more enthusiasm than they'd shown the day before. "You're here. You're here."

Lizzie remembered how Mother and Father had reacted the day before when she showed signs of confusion. No matter how she felt, she had to let things play out however they would, like a bad dream, until she could get back home. Which meant going along with whatever turn of events arose. She'd play her part.

Pasting a smile on her face, Lizzie forced a giggle. "Of course, I'm here. Where else would I be?"

She began tickling the girls until they rolled around on the bed with laughter. It helped to take their mind off of her leaving.

"I wondered what was going on." Mother stood in the doorway, her hand clasping the wooden door as she peeked in on them. "It's time to get ready for breakfast."

"You heard Mother." Lizzie straightened. "Go get ready for breakfast."

"Are we going on another adventure today?" Olivia asked.

Her body stiffened. Was she expected to take care of the girls every day? They were adorable, but Lizzie needed some peace and quiet, time to figure out her problem.

"Maybe it would be better to take a break today. After all, we had a very long day yesterday." Even Lizzie was tired.

"Aww." The girls frowned.

"Go get dressed." Lizzie ushered them to the door. "I've got to get ready, and Mother is going to be upset if our breakfast gets cold."

After closing the door, Lizzie rummaged through the dresser drawers. Didn't her great-great-grandmother own any pants? Lizzie remembered her great-grandmother telling her they didn't have closets back then, so she checked the armoire. Dresses, and more dresses. The only time Lizzie usually wore a dress was for a special occasion, or maybe a sundress in the summer.

She opted for a short-sleeve, pale green dress that looked springy, and hurried downstairs for breakfast. Lizzie's eyes widened when she saw a middle-aged woman in a white, ruffled apron, setting food on the table. They had a maid? For some reason, it made her smile. What she wouldn't give for a maid in real life.

Thinking of home made her wonder if maybe she needed to go back to her great-grandmothers to get home. She wished either of her older brothers were here. They loved science fiction and were bound to be able to help her figure this out. For now, the only thing she could think of trying was to find the location she was in before she transported back in time.

Lizzie took her seat across from her sisters at the table. Their cook placed a plate with strawberry crepes and bacon in front of her. She took a deep breath to inhale the tantalizing smell and licked her lips. "Thank you. This looks delicious."

"You're welcome, miss."

Smiling, Lizzie reached for her fork.

"Aren't you going to wait for us to pray?" Olivia frowned at her.

"Sorry." Lizzie laid her fork down and folded her hands. "I was anxious to eat so that I could run some errands."

"You don't really have time to go anywhere before church starts," Father said.

"Church?" Lizzie blinked.

It was his turn to show his displeasure as his eyes narrowed and he gave her a stern look. "It is Sunday, and we always go to church."

She started to speak, and clamped her mouth shut before telling them she normally went to church on Saturday night so that she could sleep in on Sunday. "I'm sorry. I have my days mixed up and obviously forgot today was Sunday."

That seemed to appease Father to her relief.

The hard part would be facing a church full of strangers and pretending she knew people she'd never met before.

Lizzie also needed an excuse later to go exploring, so that she could try and find her great-grandmother's house. "Will I be allowed to go for a walk alone today, or to do some sight-seeing?"

"Sightseeing?" Mother laughed. "You sound like you're visiting somewhere new."

To Lizzie, the past was new, and a little daunting.

The temperature was slightly cooler today, so Lizzie donned a jacket that reminded her of a tighter fitting sports coat that coordinated with her dress.

Mother had asked her about a hat, but Lizzie vehemently refused. She didn't care if she looked like 'a lady' or not. As she stepped outside into the cool breeze, she envisioned Mother's reaction if she could have seen Lizzie in a baseball cap and a pair of jeans with a hole in them.

Climbing into Father's black Ford Model C car made her smile, and almost want to laugh. The car didn't have a roof, or doors. It resembled a horse carriage, minus the horses, and had a small engine. So much for warming up the car before they went anywhere on a cold day. Then thoughts of snow and rain made her heart race. *Please don't let it rain today…and let me get back home, to my real home,* Lizzie added to her prayer.

Olivia and Mary Margaret scooted into the backseat with her. Thankfully, they were small. Lizzie doubted three adults could fit in the back seat. Mother and Father would be surprised if they saw a modern-day minivan, not that they were planning to have any more children. "Can I ask a question?"

"Sure, dear." Mother glanced over her shoulder at Lizzie.

"Why did you wait so long to have more children?"

"Elizabeth Ruth Ambrewster." Father's tone was curt.

The use of her full name, even if the last name wasn't really hers, was evidence enough that she'd said something wrong.

Mother laid a hand on Father's arm. A pained expression crossed his face.

"I'm sorry," Lizzie said. "I shouldn't have asked."

"It's all right, dear." Mother's voice was soft. "People don't generally talk about the children they lost before they were born, and it's especially hard to talk about when you've lost three."

Lizzie felt bad for bringing up such a delicate subject. People were more open to conversations in modern times, but they were still a sensitive subject, especially when someone had multiple miscarriages. She reached forward and laid a gentle hand on Mother's shoulder. "I'm sorry."

Mother patted her hand and nodded.

Father started the car and they rode to church in silence, not that they could have talked much over the sounds the car made, or noise of people using their horns for more than just warnings. Some people, including Father, beeped their horn to wave at someone they recognized walking, or driving down the road.

Butterflies danced in Lizzie's stomach as they parked down the street from the white-paneled church. It looked familiar, like she'd ridden past it in the future, but it'd been renovated and added on to over the years. That was a good sign at least—that the church was bound to grow. However, right now, she only knew the people she was walking in the door with and it scared her.

"Lizzie, Lillian is waving at you." Mother nudged her softly and nodded.

Lizzie followed her gaze. A bouncy blonde was smiling and waving wildly as she approached the Ambrewster family. Maybe if she had seen Lillian waving from the distance, the girl wouldn't have felt the need to come over to them. Now, Lizzie would be forced to carry on a conversation. She pasted on a smile, and pretended she knew the girl.

"Hello, Lillian." The less she said, the better.

"Hi, Lizzie." Lillian giggled. "Can I borrow her for a few minutes, Mrs. Ambrewster?"

"By all means, just make sure you both make it back inside church on time." Mother smiled. "We'll be sitting in our usual seats, Lizzie."

She assumed that was code for, *you're expected to sit with us*. Lizzie nodded.

Lillian looped her arm through Lizzie's and dragged her aside, away from earshot of anyone else.

Though startled, Lizzie obliged, leaning her head away from Lillian's frilly white hat. "I assume you wanted to tell me something?"

The girl stopped and leaned closer to Lizzie, practically squealing in her ear. "There's a new boy in church today and he is absolutely delightful."

Lizzie laughed. Not at the prospect of meeting a new boy, but at the way Lillian referenced him.

"Let me guess," Lizzie said, "you think he's cute and you want me to help find a way for you to meet him?"

"I wish." Lillian sighed. "From what I can tell, he's here to see you and looks quite dapper in his blue pinstripe suit."

"Me?" Lizzie's voice squeaked. Who in the world would be here to see her? Her expression sobered as a knot formed in the pit of her stomach. Did her great-great-grandmother have a boyfriend? Lizzie could muddle her way through some things but pretending to be infatuated with some guy she didn't know was not one of them.

"There you are."

Lizzie didn't have to turn around to recognize that playfully seductive voice. "Are you stalking me?"

"Excuse me?" Jeremiah came into view, looking at her with squinted eyes and a half-smile. "Is it wrong to want to find you so that I could apologize?"

"Church is the place for forgiveness." Lillian smiled, giggling like a nervous school girl.

"Why are you rolling your eyes?" Jeremiah's brows furrowed. "At least that's what it looks like you are doing."

She almost chuckled. Her mother accused her of doing that on numerous occasions.

"I'm sorry." Lizzie sighed. "And Lillian is right, I shouldn't hold a grudge. It's not my place to judge how many women you flirt with."

"I don't flirt." A flicker of pain shone in his brown eyes. "I have to be polite to people when I'm working."

"Which includes going home to dinner with them?" She could hear the accusation in her own tone. "I'm sorry. It's none of my business what you do on your free time." Guilt niggled her. "And I appreciate you taking a good part of your day yesterday to help me and my sisters. That was very kind of you."

Jeremiah smiled. "You can be the most infuriating and quizzical woman all in the same breath."

"And yet you're smiling." Lizzie grinned. Men in this era were an odd bunch. She found it hard to remain upset with him, even though her head knew she had no reason to be upset to begin with. He had a certain charm. "So, tell me, Jeremiah. What brought you to our church today?"

"You." His brown eyes held her captive.

Her breath caught. "How did you know I would be here—at this church?"

"Fate."

Lizzie's cheeks warmed.

"We'd better hurry in or we'll be late for service." Lillian nudged Lizzie. "And I promised your mother we would be on time."

"Shall we?" Jeremiah extended the crook of his arm for Lizzie to hold onto as they walked.

That was one thing she wished men still did today, well, in modern times. She liked the close, almost possessive feeling of walking into church on his arm. It didn't escape her attention that a couple girls gasped, envy evident on several girl's faces.

A rush of exhilaration coursed through her. Lizzie reminded herself that she and Jeremiah were only friends, and to think otherwise was foolish. He had a charismatic way that made girls swoon. She wasn't feeble, or easily charmed.

Lizzie leaned closer to Jeremiah and lowered her voice. "My parents are over there."

He followed the direction of her nod, stopping at the end of the pew. He allowed her to slide in next to her family before taking a seat next to her. Jeremiah leaned forward and reached in front of her to shake Father's hand. "Hello. Nice to meet you, Sir. I'm Jeremiah Hopkins."

Music began to play as people bustled toward their seats.

Father shook his hand. "I look forward to speaking with you after service."

Jeremiah leaned back in his seat and winked at Lizzie.

Her heart pounded, reminding her that she was still breathing—albeit a little breathlessly.

Chapter Ten

After church, Lizzie had the opportunity to properly introduce Jeremiah to Father and Mother. Lizzie had hoped to make introductions, and then make an excuse for them to go to lunch and on a walk. She wanted Jeremiah to help her find her grandmother's house.

Father had other plans, like inviting Jeremiah over for lunch so that they could get acquainted.

Olivia and Mary Margaret both petitioned Father to sit by Jeremiah at the dinner table—Olivia won. Lizzie smiled when Father asked Jeremiah to say grace. To her surprise, Jeremiah did so without hesitation.

"What's this?" Lizzie asked, pointing to the plate Miss Ella placed in front of her. She'd only learned the woman's name from hearing the girls address her in conversation.

Miss Ella's eyebrow arched a fraction. "Parsnips, miss."

"Ah, thank you. It looks delicious." Lizzie didn't mention she was referring to the roast, potatoes, and carrots. She'd never had parsnips. Sprinkling a dash of salt on her vegetables, Lizzie took a small bite of the parsnip. To her surprise, it tasted a little sweet, and salty.

She looked up from her plate to see Jeremiah smiling at her. Something in the way he looked at her made her cheeks warm.

"What do you do for a living?" Father asked, distracting them from the moment between them.

Jeremiah wiped his mouth with the cloth napkin from his lap, then returned it before looking Father squarely in the face. "I'm a conductor, sir. Have been for the past year and a half."

"I see."

The way he said it gave Lizzie the impression he didn't approve. She didn't know why she felt the need to support Jeremiah, but she did. "I think it'd be a fun job. Getting to ride the train from city to city, seeing different states and tourist attractions between shifts."

"Tourist attractions?" Mother laughed. "There you go with those fancy thoughts of yours again. Honestly, Lizzie, I don't know what's gotten into you lately."

"I have an idea," Father said in a deep tone. He directed his attention toward Jeremiah again. "Do you have any bigger aspirations?"

Jeremiah shrugged nonchalantly. "I think riding the rails is a fine profession. Sometimes I make extra money by buying things from one place and selling them in another."

"We have stores and catalogues to order from for such things," Father said.

Lips pursed, Jeremiah's nose jutted up a fraction. "That's true, but not everything is in a catalogue and not everyone can travel."

"I want to travel," Olivia announced. "Do you think they have animals in Heaven? Miss Chamblee said we will all get to go to Heaven one day." She smiled, wide-eyed, at Jeremiah. "Do they have a train that goes there? Maybe we can take another adventure?"

"Another adventure?" Father's brows furrowed as he glanced from Olivia to Lizzie.

Mother's eyes became teary.

Lizzie remembered their conversation on the way to church, and thought of Mother's unborn children, already in Heaven. Her heart raced. "Olivia, we'll discuss Heaven later. Did you tell Father about all the things we saw when we went to see the progress on the fair?" Lizzie's smile was shaky. "Did you tell him about the World's Fair Flight Cage? One day it will be part of the St. Louis Zoo."

"St. Louis doesn't have a zoo," Father said.

"It will eventually," Lizzie insisted, "and it all started because of the walk-through flight cage."

"What is going to fly in this cage, and what makes you think it will cause the city to want to build a zoo?" Father scoffed. "Surely they wouldn't want dangerous animals so close to where people lived. What if they got out?"

Lizzie sighed. What use was it trying to tell them of things to come. To her, it was exciting to see what things used to be like, especially knowing what the future held.

She didn't dare ask what he thought might 'fly' in the cage, such as a pterodactyl. Were they even aware of prehistorical creatures? Taking a deep breath, she decided to explain the exhibit to him, like she would a small child. "The caged enclosure will have a fenced in tunnel for people to walk through and see the birds up closer."

"Birds aren't dangerous," Father admitted, "but that doesn't explain why you think there will be a zoo. There's never been mention of anyone planning to build one in this city to my knowledge."

With Father being a banker, he was prone to knowing what businesses, or even the city, borrowed money for.

"I guess time will tell." Lizzie chuckled. Their skepticism would fade eventually. Hopefully, she would be back in her timeline before that happened.

When they finished their meal, Lizzie stood and picked up her dishes to take to the kitchen. "Jeremiah and I are going to go for a long walk."

"I know it has warmed up a little, but you still need to wear a jacket," Mother said.

Father's frown of disapproval was obvious, and he didn't appear to care if he hid his dissatisfaction. "I'd like to speak with you a moment, Lizzie. Perhaps Jeremiah could wait outside?"

Jeremiah rose, and nodded toward Father. "Thank you for having me over, Mrs. Russell. Please tell your cook that the food was delicious." He shook hands with Father. "Thank you, sir."

"You're welcome." Father shook his hand and waited until Jeremiah had gone before addressing Lizzie. "I would like to enquire into the nature of your relationship with this young man?"

"My relationship?" Lizzie almost laughed. Instead, she shrugged. "We're friends."

"So, you have no inclinations for him?" Father's arms were crossed in front of him. He peered down over the rim of his glasses at her.

She chuckled. "If you mean feelings, no, and if I did, so what?"

"I would expect you to want to seek someone with more aspirations." There was no mistaking the disdain in his voice.

"Jeremiah has an honest job and he works hard, so who cares what he does?" The hairs on the back of Lizzie's neck stood up. Apparently, snobs existed in the past, and hadn't changed a whole lot in the future either, which infuriated her to no end. "Besides, I'm a grown woman. I think you should trust me to make decisions about whom I choose to date, or marry, myself."

Father sighed. Pain etched his eyes. "I don't wish to see you get hurt or be left unprovided for."

He cared for his daughter. If this wasn't a dream, then her great-great-grandmother would hopefully assume the role of herself—and soon, so perhaps it was best that Lizzie didn't cause her any undo grief by starting a family feud. Her mind felt jumbled again with questions that she didn't have answers to. If she was in her great-great-grandmother's body, then where was her great-great-grandmother?

This wasn't the home her great-grandmother, or grandmother lived in, which is why she hoped she could find the house. Maybe it was the key to going back to her timeline?

If her great-great-grandmother had switched places with her, she was probably enjoying the time to get to see her future daughter and granddaughter. That thought gave Lizzie some comfort.

"Thank you for your concern, Father. I can assure you I am not looking to marry, or date, anyone in the near future."

"You don't know how relieved we are to hear you say that." Mother sounded chipper. "Mrs. Adams would like for you to meet her grandson when he comes to visit her in June."

Lizzie rolled her eyes but didn't comment. "I best hurry. Jeremiah is waiting outside." At least she hoped he hadn't left without her. She scurried toward the door, still feeling restrained by wearing such a long dress.

When she opened the front door, Jeremiah quickly turned around. "I wasn't sure if you would be joining me."

She laughed. "I guess you could tell Father was being a bit protective."

"He's a learned man." Jeremiah frowned. "I imagine he expects someone equally educated for his daughters."

"Let's hope he's not trying to marry my sisters off already." Lizzie giggled like a school girl, then blushed as she realized how *girlie* she sounded. This timeline was beginning to seriously mess with her, including how she thought and acted. She needed to get back to her reality before she ended up trapped.

"What's wrong?" Jeremiah took hold of her forearms. "Are you having doubts about spending the day with me?"

Shaking her head, Lizzie forced a smile. "No, there are other things bothering me." She swallowed. "Can we take a walk and talk about it? There's a place I need to find."

"I'll be happy to help."

She told him her grandmother's address.

"I know where that is." He took her hand and guided her down the street. "It's maybe six or so blocks away."

Part of her wanted to tell Jeremiah about her dilemma, but he might think she was crazy, and wouldn't agree to help her. She didn't know what else to talk about. It occurred to her that she knew very little about him, other than where he worked and lived. She'd also met his aunt. "So, tell me about yourself."

He smiled. "I have a brother named Nehemiah, who is twenty-one, and my sister, Ruth, is eighteen."

"Let me guess," Lizzie said, "biblical names?"

"Yes." His teeth were pearly white, even though they didn't have teeth whitener back then. Lizzie liked the way his eyes sparkled as he talked about his siblings.

"I take it you all get along well?"

"Of course, we do." Jeremiah's brows furrowed. "You get along with your siblings, too, so why does that surprise you?"

"They're closer to your own age." Lizzie shrugged. "I guess I thought…" She almost said she thought they would squabble like she did with her brothers but caught herself. "I don't know. Anyhow, continue. Tell me what made you want to become a conductor."

"As I said at dinner, I wanted to see the world." He gently bumped shoulders with her as his eyes locked with hers. "And you can't do that in a classroom."

She knew how he felt. When she was younger, she wanted to take a year off before going to college, but her parents encouraged her to go and get it over with, or they said she might end up not going at all. Plus, she'd risk losing her scholarships. "Are you thinking of ever going to college?"

"Not everyone goes, Lizzie." He stared ahead. "It's very expensive."

"It is, but it can also help you get a better job." Now she sounded like Father. "I'm sorry. It's not any of my business. You should do whatever makes you happy."

Jeremiah grinned. "If I did that, then I would kiss you."

Chapter Eleven

Lizzie tried to ignore the words Jeremiah had said on their way to her great-grandmother's property, but her mind kept imagining what his kisses might taste like. Distracted by her rampant thoughts, she stumbled over a crack in the sidewalk. When he reached to steady her, his fingertips felt like fire and she jumped at his touch. "I'm fine."

She felt anything but fine. Especially when they reached their destination. The empty lot in front of her was clearer than her jumbled mind. "It's not here."

"What were you expecting?" Jeremiah looked from Lizzie to the grass covered property in front of them.

"My great-grandmother's home." A disappointing swoosh of air escaped from her lungs.

"Maybe they tore it down?"

She almost laughed. The chances were, it probably hadn't been built yet.

"Can I tell you something," Lizzie asked, "and you promise not to think I'm crazy?"

"I would never think you were out of your mind." Jeremiah's expression sobered.

"I know this is going to sound like something out of a science fiction movie…" Lizzie remembered they didn't have television. She paced frantically, then stopped in front of Jeremiah and stared into his wide, brown eyes. "I'm sorry. I don't know how to say this, but I'm not from here."

A smile etched the corner of his lips. "Are you playing games with me again?"

Lizzie slowly shook her head. "A few days ago, I was visiting my grandmother and my great-grandmother—they live together, and Great-grandma Mullane showed me the Crazy Quilt, that was the name of it, that her mother had made." She took a deep breath and continued, "I laid down with the quilt and fell asleep. When I woke, I was here." Lizzie held her hands out, palms extended upward. "Back in the time of my great-great-grandmother. Somehow, I seem to have taken her place or something."

Taking a calming breath, Lizzie closed her eyes.

Jeremiah's arms embraced her.

She relaxed, laying her head on his shoulder, smelling the spicy scent of his cologne. "I just want to get back home, but I don't know how."

"I'll help you find a way," Jeremiah promised.

Savoring the comfort of his arms, she absorbed the warmth his body offered, slowly nodded in recognition of his promise.

"Thank you." Her response was barely more than a whisper, but he'd obviously heard her because he held Lizzie even closer.

Several moments of silence lingered, before she lifted her head off his shoulder.

Jeremiah tilted her chin upward to look at her. His thumb gently brushed against her cheek. "From everything you've told me, we know that you can't go back to your great-grandmother's."

Lizzie already knew that, because there wasn't a house and it would be years before one was built.

"So, what about the quilt?" Jeremiah asked. "Maybe you have to make it like she did? Then you can get home."

"Maybe." Frustration welled up in Lizzie like a volcano, threatening to explode. "However, I don't know how to sew."

"So, you learn."

She wanted to laugh at how nonchalantly he thought the task would be. "And who do you suppose I get to teach me?"

"Your mother didn't strike me as the type of woman to make her own clothing." Jeremiah's lips pressed together to the side, and his pupils raised as his mind apparently grasped for ideas.

It was mesmerizing to watch him process his thoughts. The closeness made her a little uncomfortable. She wiggled out of his embrace and began to pace, long enough to put a couple feet between them.

"You could join a sewing group," he suggested. "I think some churches or women's groups may have them. If not, I could ask my sister if she would come and stay with you for a few days."

"A few days?" Lizzie's eyes widened. "You think I can learn that quickly?"

"You certainly have the motivation to try." Jeremiah smiled.

That, she did. Lizzie remembered the fabric in the chair in her bedroom that her sister had pointed out the morning she woke up in this place. It was all the same material, and the original quilt had five different fabrics. "But there's still another problem. I have to find the exact fabrics my great-great-grandmother used."

"I'm off work tomorrow," Jeremiah beamed. "We can go shopping together."

"But don't you live in St. Louis?"

Jeremiah nodded. "I have a friend that I can stay with."

"Thanks." Lizzie smiled. "Maybe we could also check out a few stores today as well?"

"You really aren't from here, are you?" Laughter bellowed as his chest shook. "Blue laws forbid some businesses to be open, or for some things to be sold on the sabbath."

"That's right." Lizzie snapped her fingers and pointed at Jeremiah. "I remember my grandmother telling me that they couldn't sell soda on Sunday either and that's how the ice cream sundae came about."

His eyes squinted as he looked at her curiously. "So, things change in the future?"

"Oh, yeah, a lot." Lizzie laughed. "Wait until you get to try concretes."

Jeremiah scrunched his face in a peculiar distortion of disapproval. "They'll have edible sidewalks?" He shook his head. "That sounds disgusting. Who would want to eat something you walked on?"

Her cheeks hurt from smiling so wide. Clearly, it would take more effort to explain the future. She imagined it much like speaking Christianese to a non-Christian. They would be clueless. Which was why the book of Revelations was so hard for her to understand. When John wrote the Revelations, he was talking about things that were yet to come—the future. So, he obviously didn't know how to describe modern things that hadn't happened yet with the proper terminology.

"You don't walk on it, silly." Lizzie let out a deep breath. "But I can see how the name could be confusing. I think they call it a concrete because it is thick." She shrugged and chuckled. "I guess it really is an odd thing to call ice cream, but it is delicious."

"I'll have to take your word for that." His hands in his pockets, he stared at her.

Goosebumps ran up Lizzie spine and she shivered.

"Are you cold?" He started to take off his suit coat, until she shook her head.

"I'm fine." At least she was physically. Emotionally was another story. "All this talk about ice cream made me cold and hungry for dessert. You really should try ice cream with chocolate candy mixed in."

"When the weather gets warmer, we'll have to give it a try." Jeremiah closed the gap between them and entwined his arm in hers. "In the meantime, why don't we go get a cup of tea?"

Jeremiah led Lizzie toward a busier street not far from the train station. The restaurant he took her to reminded her more of a café. It was old, yet modern, given that for their era, it was relatively new. Things still confused Lizzie, like the realization that the old soda fountains and paintings on the walls were not restorations or reproductions—they were the originals.

After their earlier conversation, she laughed secretly at the sign in front of the soda fountains that informed patrons no soda would be sold on Sunday. Lizzie knew better than ask for iced coffee after their meal at the fair. She was certain iced tea came about years before anyone started drinking iced coffee. "Can I have a cup of coffee with cream?"

"Sure." Jeremiah took change out of his pocket and handed it to the cashier. "Can I get two cups of coffee with milk?"

Milk? Lizzie groaned inwardly. Creamer probably hadn't been invented yet. She took a seat near the window. Jeremiah carried their cups of coffee to the table, placing one in front of her before sitting in the wooden chair across from her.

"I didn't think to bring my purse," Lizzie said, realizing she'd allowed him to pay for her beverage. This wasn't a date. He was a friend, helping her. "I'll pay you back, I promise."

"No need." He took a sip of his coffee. His eyes remained focused on her the whole time. "A gentleman never allows a lady to pay."

Granted, the coffee didn't cost that much, but it made her feel beholden to him. Why didn't men like this exist in her timeline? Today, guys often expected something in return if they were paying your way, and they definitely didn't talk and act as refined. It was one of the few things she'd found enchanting about this era.

Movement outside the window caught her attention. A middle-aged couple strolled along the sidewalk, the woman holding onto the man's arm at the elbow. The sight of her pale blue striped dress with little pink and white flowers with green leaves made Lizzie's breath catch.

"That's it," she muttered, pointing toward the retreating figure.

Jeremiah turned to look.

Lizzie stood and hurried out the door in pursuit of the couple. "Ma'am, please wait."

The woman glanced over her shoulder, verifying she was the one being summoned.

To Lizzie's relief, the woman stopped.

The man with her looked slightly confused, until he caught sight of Lizzie. "Can we help you?"

She nodded. "Your dress. I need that fabric."

"I beg your pardon?" The woman's eyes widened as her hand flew to her chest.

"I'm sorry." Lizzie giggled at how her words must have sounded to the lady. "I'm making a very important quilt and I need to find that fabric to use. Can you tell me where you got your dress, or the fabric if it was handmade?"

"It was a gift from my sister," the woman said. "She ordered it from a catalogue."

Jeremiah had joined them, nodding to the man when he approached.

"Do you know what catalogue?" There could be dozens of catalogues. How would she know which one? "Or even if you could tell me the name of the store that carries the dress?"

The woman shook her head. "I'm sorry. My sister is visiting relatives in London."

"Can you call her?" Lizzie's voice squeaked.

"I'm afraid not, dear." The woman frowned. "While we do have a telephone, we don't have the ability to call overseas."

"When will she be back?" Panic gripped her heart tighter than a vice grip.

"We don't expect her back for a couple of months," the man informed Lizzie. "I'm sorry that we're not able to help you."

They turned to go.

Lizzie reached out, grabbing the woman's arm firmer than she'd intended. "Please, can I buy the dress from you? Anything? I really need that material."

"Please unhand my wife, or I'll be forced to call the constable."

"I'm sorry. I assure you that won't be necessary." Jeremiah wrapped his arm around Lizzie's waist and urged her to move away from the couple. "Come on, Lizzie. We'll figure something out."

As her hand loosened her grip on the woman's arm, Lizzie felt her chances of creating the exact same quilt slipping out of her grasp as well. She had to get home—she just had to!

Chapter Twelve

Monday morning after breakfast, and Father had gone to work, Lizzie and Jeremiah set off on foot to find the fabric for the quilt at what Jeremiah referred to as a dry goods store. Given the past didn't have modern refrigeration, it made sense to refer to a store as something quirky as that.

"I get the feeling your parents don't like me."

Expelling a long breath, Lizzie shook her head. She had omitted telling Father that Jeremiah would be escorting her today. The look of disapproval Mother gave that morning when Jeremiah showed up at their home was confirmation enough that she'd done the right thing by not telling Father. It wasn't as if she and Jeremiah were planning to run away and get married…

Lizzie's heart pounded, and her ears rang. Her head jerked toward Jeremiah. "It's you."

"Me?" Jeremiah's narrowed. He frowned. "What did I do wrong? I'd be happy to apologize."

She grinned.

"Are you laughing at me?" He stopped in his tracks. His cheeks reddened. "I don't know why you find this all amusing."

"I'm not laughing at you." Lizzie tried to hide her smile. "I just remembered something my great-grandmother said to me." It was Lizzie's turn for her cheeks to turn red.

"Now you're embarrassed." Jeremiah took a step closer and tilted her chin up. His chocolate-brown eyes searched hers. "What did your great-grandmother say?"

"I...," Lizzie stammered. "I remembered one of the fabrics, it was dark blue. Like your uniform."

Jeremiah smiled. "So, you're saying I was important to her?"

Her, being her great-great-grandmother, yes. But he was vastly becoming important to Lizzie too. It was easy to get lost in the depth of his gaze. She moistened her lips and tried to swallow. "Yes. However, something happened to come between them."

He grimaced. "Like she went back to the future and left him all alone?"

"No." She nervously shook her head. "All I know is, something came between them and she was heartbroken. She later married someone else."

"I can't imagine anything coming between us...other than your father."

Lizzie's eyes felt weighted by sadness. "Surely he could see that his daughter's happiness is more important than whether or not her boyfriend has a college degree?"

A smile crept upon his lips. "So, I'm your boyfriend now?"

She playfully punched his arm.

His eyes widened in surprise as he laughed. "You hit me."

"Be nice, or I'll do it again." Lizzie turned to walk away so he wouldn't see her grinning from ear-to-ear. She felt like a silly schoolgirl.

"Well, with an attitude like that, I may not be willing to give you the fabric for your quilt."

Pausing in her steps, she swiveled to look at him, relaxing slightly when she saw the playful look on his face. "Perhaps you have a co-worker, whom I might be able to persuade."

Jeremiah shook his head. "It won't work. You said yourself, she used the fabric from someone she was in love with."

It would serve him right if she wiped that smug look off of his face, but he was right, and she was falling for him.

Another thought haunted her. What if she were the reason her great-great-grandmother didn't get married to him? How she wished she knew the whole story.

Friday evening, Lizzie met Ruth at the train station as promised. Ruth exerted the same bubbly and fun personality traits as her brother. She even had the same dark brown hair, playful brown eyes, and cute narrow nose. The teen stood at least two inches shorter than Lizzie. Clutched in her hands was a rugged, rustic brown trunk that had seen better days. It reminded Lizzie of a smaller trunk she'd kept valuables locked away in at college, except this one was old, with leather straps.

"That must be heavy?" Lizzie nodded toward the case. "Too bad it doesn't have wheels on it."

"You and your ideas." Jeremiah chuckled. "I'm curious though, how did you get your father to agree to let Ruth come spend the weekend with you?"

"I told him since he was uncomfortable with our friendship, then perhaps it would be better if I spent time with your sister instead. Plus, she was willing to teach me how to sew, and he thought that was a good idea." Lizzie smirked. "Seems he could be persuaded that it may be a trait one might want to use in the future, should they wish to marry."

Lizzie omitted the part of the conversation with her father that entailed his questioning that those intentions had nothing to do with Jeremiah. That discussion was a battle for another day.

"Anyhow, Father is waiting in the car." Lizzie bit her lower lip. "Ruth and I should join him."

The look of dejection on Jeremiah's face made Lizzie's heart ache.

"I understand." Always the gentleman, Jeremiah didn't voice his disappointment. His eyes brightened a little. "I do have a gift for you."

"You do?" Lizzie asked.

Ruth beamed, nodding in agreement.

A corner of Jeremiah's mouth lifted in a lopsided grin. "My sister will give it to you tomorrow."

"Tomorrow?" Lizzie sulked. "Why do I have to wait?"

"Same thing I asked myself." Jeremiah laughed heartily. "But as they say, good things come to those who wait."

Saturday morning, Mary Margaret and Olivia insisted on needing to learn to sew. Ruth was a good sport and said she would be happy to teach them as well. Mother said she was going to read in the sitting room while she listened to music and for the girls to have fun.

Not that sewing was on Lizzie's list of enjoyable things to do, she was excited to spend time with Jeremiah's sister. Ruth possessed a naïve innocence that Lizzie treasured. The past held a certain wonder and excitement, even if there were fewer things to do without the convenience of electronics. Getting accustomed to the phonograph and outdated music took some time. The lyrics reflected the virtue of the era, especially when the top song from the previous year was *In the Good Old Summer Time*. It amazed Lizzie how many songs had trees in them.

"I can't wait to see what Jeremiah's surprise is," Lizzie whispered next to Ruth's ear as she and the girls headed to Lizzie's room.

Squeals of excitement bubbled out of Ruth. She grabbed the small trunk of her belongings and hoisted it on Lizzie's bed. Ruth sneakily reached into it and pulled out what appeared to be a magazine.

Lizzie stared at it, slowly reaching out to take it from Ruth. "What's this?"

"Jeremiah said you wanted to look through it for fabrics." Ruth sighed and reached into her trunk again. "Perhaps you'll like this better?" She handed Lizzie a pair of Jeremiah's work trousers. "He caught them on something and they have a small rip, but that'll be fine since we were going to have to cut them up for the quilt anyway."

"They're perfect." Lizzie beamed, grabbing the trousers from Ruth and clutching them to her chest. "Now I just have to find the other five fabrics."

During the next two hours, Ruth helped Lizzie design the flower pattern she needed for the quilt. They cut out sample pieces to use as a guide to cut the shapes she needed once she found the remaining fabric.

Finally came the time to learn to actually sew. Mary Margaret and Olivia anxiously held their fabric swatches in their tiny hands.

"Now you want to be very careful," Ruth instructed them. "The needle is very sharp, and you don't want to poke yourself." She pointed to the tip of the needle, then she explained how to thread the needle and tie a knot in the end. "You want to put the right side of the fabric together so that you actually sew the back side of the material."

"How do you know which is the right side?" Olivia asked, flipping the fabric back and forth.

Ruth gave a lopsided grin, remaining patient as she was amused with her young, captive audience. "See this side?"

The girls nodded. So, did Lizzie.

"The color of the fabric isn't as vibrant on the back side of the material as it is on the front side."

Given they were working with samples of white material, it was harder to tell.

Ruth must have sensed their confusion. She set her fabric samples on the bed and turned up the end of her peach floral dress. "Here, maybe you can tell better by looking at a print fabric."

Sure enough, the underside of her dress was lighter. Lizzie turned her dress up and looked at the other side. She laughed when her sisters did the same.

"Thank you for all of your help and patience in explaining this to us, Ruth." She hugged Jeremiah's sister. "I can't tell you how much I appreciate it."

"It's fine," Ruth said. "I'm happy to help. In fact, I'm thinking of entering a quilt in the contest at the World's Fair too."

By the time Ruthie left Monday morning, Lizzie felt she had a good grasp on how to stitch two pieces of fabric together, and then add the next piece, and so on, until she had a complete quilt square.

Ruth promised she'd come back again to help Lizzie when she was ready to assemble the pieces—provided Lizzie could find the fabrics she needed. If she didn't, she might never make it back home.

Chapter Thirteen

May 1904

Lizzie and Jeremiah had worked out a routine. She would take a walk around the time Jeremiah's train came through the Warrensburg Train Depot so that she could see him a few brief minutes. Then on his days off, Ruth sometimes tagged along so that Lizzie's father wouldn't suspect anything. Ruth may not have started out as Lizzie's friend, but she'd quickly become one.

The Tuesday after Mother's Day, Jeremiah gave Lizzie another catalogue when she came to see him.

"Thank you."

"You're welcome." He smiled at her, holding her gaze captive by his mesmerizing brown eyes. "How did your mother like her present?"

"She was a little confused as to why I was giving her a gift when it wasn't her birthday or Christmas." How was Lizzie to know they didn't celebrate Mother's Day yet? "But she definitely loved the dragonfly brooch you gave me to give her." Sadness weighed heavily on her heart. "I wish I could have told her that it was from you."

"It was from both of us." Jeremiah playfully tipped the end of her nose with his finger. "And one day, we'll be able to tell her. After we convince your parents I'm not a bad sort."

Lizzie smiled. "That you're not."

The train whistle blew, signaling it would be departing soon.

"I hate saying goodbye."

"Me too." Lizzie hugged the catalogue to her chest and looked wistfully away. "Even though we did just get to spend yesterday together."

Movement caught her attention as Jeremiah quickly kissed her cheek, her turning her head caused his lips to brush hers instead. For a moment, he lingered. "I look forward to seeing you again tomorrow."

She nodded, afraid to trust her words.

With a wave, Jeremiah retreated up the steps and back to work.

Lizzie sighed. In a daze, she walked home. When she went inside, she heard chatter coming from the parlor. She followed the sound of the voices. "Lillian?"

"Hello, Lizzie." Lillian stood to face her.

"How are you?" Lizzie asked. She'd seen the girl two days ago at church, so why was she here?

"Well…" Lillian bit her lower lip and looked at Mother.

"Come have a seat, Lizzie." Mother patted the seat next to her on the sofa.

She did as she was instructed, smoothing out her dress as she sat, then she folded her hands in her lap. It didn't take a genius to figure out she was being cornered. Otherwise, it was some sort of intervention.

Mother's features were soft, yet firm as she locked eyes with Lizzie. "You've been rather preoccupied lately. In fact, your father and I were under the impression that you'd been spending time with Lillian lately."

Lizzie shrugged. When possible, she avoided saying whom she was spending time with, if anyone.

"Lillian has been your friend for a very long time and she misses you."

How could she tell them that she really didn't know Lillian?

Olivia poked an inquisitive tilted, head around the parlor doorway, her tiny hand holding on to the white wooden trim. "May I come in?"

"Not now," Mother said, giving her a stern look.

A frown formed on Olivia's face, before alarm registered in her wide eyes as she lost her balance and tumbled to the floor.

Everyone giggled once they realized Olivia wasn't hurt.

Lizzie's jaw slumped. "Your dress."

Olivia looked at her dress. "Is it ripped?"

"No. Your dress is fine." Lizzie shook her head. "The fabric, that's exactly what I need for my quilt."

To her surprise, Olivia shook her head vehemently. "You're not cutting up my dress."

"I...," Lizzie stammered. How did you convince a five-year-old the importance of sacrifice? Olivia would never agree to it if she knew it was so Lizzie could get back home.

"Now, you know that I told you earlier that this is the last time you can wear that dress," Mother said. "It's getting too short. Look." Mother pointed. "I can start to see your knees."

Her sister leaned forward to look, which made her dress look longer when she bent over.

Lizzie wanted to smile, but she was more anxious in what Mother had to say. She'd been here a month and a half, and other than the background fabric, including the dark blue needed for the center of the flowers, Lizzie hadn't been able to acquire any of the material needed for the petals.

"It is rather short," Lizzie said. *It wasn't a lie*, she told herself. For the early 1900s, it was short. "Mother, do you think I could use her dress to make my quilt?"

"I'm making a quilt, too." Lillian's sounded excited and bubbly.

Some mornings, there wasn't enough coffee to deal with perky people.

"Maybe we can work on ours together?" Lillian suggested.

The proverbial shoe dropped. Lillian's complaining to Mother about Lizzie not spending time with her, and Lillian zeroing in on her opportunity.

What could Lizzie say?

Working with Lillian meant she'd have someone to help her, but it also meant she might be discovered for who she really was. Best friends knew those kind of things—didn't they?

"That sounds perfect." Mother clasped her hands together.

"But what about me?" Olivia's bottom lip curled in a pout. "Shouldn't they have to take me out for the day if they want my dress? That way, my dress and I can have one last fun day together."

"I'm sure that can be arranged," Lizzie said, happy that her youngest sister wasn't beyond bribery. "Provided Mother approves."

When Mother agreed, Olivia jumped up and down, causing her curly brown hair to bounce with her movements.

Lizzie's heart melted at her sister's excitement. She treasured this time to experience having sisters. Her brothers would have pounced on her or blackmailed her forever if they knew she wanted something.

"We could go for a walk in the park, and then stop for lunch." Lillian clasped her hands. Her face lit up with excitement. It was hard to tell who was more excited—Lillian or Olivia.

"Do you have a ball or something we could play with at the park?" Lizzie asked.

"I could take my dolly for a stroll." Olivia ran off before Lizzie could respond.

She was a bit too old to be pushing a doll around or playing with one. Playing ball would keep them active enough that she wouldn't have to talk in depth with Lillian. Lizzie's smile quivered as she stood. "We could take a picnic lunch."

"That's a wonderful idea." Lillian stood. "I'll help you prepare it."

While Lillian and Lizzie sat on a black wrought iron bench, Olivia knelt on a blanket in the grass and played with her doll, Miss Mayberry. Olivia thought Miss Mayberry might be cold, so she put a sweater on her and wrapped her in a pink blanket.

Lizzie smiled.

"I've told you all about the quilt that I am making," Lillian said. "Tell me about yours."

She shrugged. "It is going to have three different color flowers with five petals. The center of the flowers—" Lizzie paused, not wanting to tell Lillian about Jeremiah, in case the girl couldn't keep a secret. "I'm using some dark blue fabric that a friend gave me."

"A friend?" Tears welled up in her eyes. "Is that why you haven't had time for me?"

"No." Lizzie shook her head and sighed. "I've met someone, but Father doesn't approve because he doesn't have a college degree."

"A boy?" Lillian's eyes lit up. "And you've been keeping him a secret?" Lillian squealed. "You should know it's safe to tell me about him, Elizabeth Ruth Ambrewster."

Unfortunately, she didn't know, and she didn't like her full name being used, or being called by her great-great-grandmother's last name. "Well, I'm telling you now, and he has a sister named Ruth."

Lillian became like an animated child whom you'd just told them they were getting a puppy. "Her name is the same as your middle name." Her face contorted into a frown. "You aren't making this up, are you?"

Lizzie shook her head. "No, and Ruth agreed to help me learn how to sew, which has also given us an excuse for her brother to be around."

"You know..." A smile creased Lillian's face. "...if he happened to have a brother or a friend my age, we could tell your parents that he was courting me and that he had to help chaperone. That way you could also be my chaperone. Then we could all go out on adventures together. Think of all the fun we would have."

Her great-great-grandmother's friend was incorrigible. Lillian was funny and very likeable. "Jeremiah has a friend in town that he stays with sometimes. Perhaps I could see if he would introduce the two of you."

Without warning, Lillian's arms flew around Lizzie. She was giddier than a kid at Christmas. "Thank you."

Lizzie hoped she wouldn't come to regret her decision to fix Lillian up with one of Jeremiah's friends. Hopefully he would realize it was for his benefit as well as Lizzie's.

Chapter Fourteen

July 4, 1904

Lillian joined Lizzie's family on their overnight trip to the World's Fair for the fourth of July. They'd even talked Father into letting them spend the afternoon with Lillian's male suitor, who happened to be Jeremiah's friend, Thomas.

Lizzie hadn't known any other blind dates to work out before, but Thomas and Lillian were suited for each other. His wide-eyed innocence and boisterous enthusiasm mirrored Lizzie's personality. With the two of them dating for the past month, made it easier for Lizzie to see Jeremiah.

Although, once Father realized that Thomas was Jeremiah's friend, he gave Lizzie a disapproving look. More than a hundred years later, fathers would still be giving their children those looks, but it wouldn't be as affective. Which is why Lizzie so easily shirked it off. Her great-great-grandmother's happiness could be at stake, but how would that change her future? If she never made it back, she'd be doomed to live out this life—which became less and less gloomy every day.

She squeezed the small wrapped box in her right hand as she and Lillian headed down to the hotel lobby to meet Jeremiah and Thomas. Jeremiah turned twenty-three today. His birthday was what motivated her a few weeks ago to beg Father to go to the fair for the holiday. The promise of a wonderful fireworks display was all it took to convince Mary Margaret and Olivia to help persuade him. Lizzie waited nearly a week after Father had agreed to suggest that Lillian come along. Mother had been so happy that the girls were spending time again, she petitioned Father to give in—even though this was supposed to be a family trip.

"There they are," Lillian practically squealed. "Thomas is so handsome."

Thomas and Jeremiah were both dressed in charcoal gray suits, something Lizzie had grown accustomed to. She wished she had the ability to make or buy Jeremiah a pair of blue jeans. He would have been more comfortable than wearing a suit all day in the heat—not that she enjoyed wearing a long dress either, although the navy-blue dress with white lace was fitting for the holiday. She'd pared it with a small red reticule, making her ensemble even more patriotic.

"Hello," Jeremiah was the first to speak. He greeted her with a kiss on the cheek, then smiled and put his hands in his trousers. "How are both of you today?"

Lizzie's face warmed. She couldn't help smiling like a silly school girl. Her hand with the present darted out awkwardly. "Happy Birthday."

"Thank you." Jeremiah accepted the present and hugged her.

"That's right," Thomas said. "How could I forget it was your birthday? It's not like thousands of people have come here to celebrate with you at the fair."

Everyone chuckled.

"And instead of birthday candles, you'll have fireworks." Lizzie wished she could have made Jeremiah a cake. Perhaps they'd stumble across a place that sold cupcakes today.

"Open your present." Lillian beamed. You would have thought the gift was for her.

Lizzie had fun keeping the actual gift a secret, refusing to give Lillian any hints, or tell her unless she guessed the right answer. The closest she'd come to guessing was to suggest it was cufflinks.

Thomas and Lillian stared intently as Jeremiah carefully removed the blue and white wrapping paper from the box. The wide-eyed enthusiasm and innocence of her friends was endearing.

Jeremiah's jaw dropped, and his eyes widened when he took the lid off the box. He pulled out the silver pocket watch she'd given him.

"I don't know what to say... It's incredible." Warmth filled his eyes. "Thank you."

For a moment time stood still as their gazes locked. She saw love in his eyes, the same love she felt in her heart. In the past three months, they'd transitioned from total strangers on a train, to falling in love. It wasn't something she meant to happen, but it did.

If she were honest with herself, she'd admit that her only desire to work on the quilt any more was to have adventures to go on with Jeremiah in search of their conquest for the other fabrics. She enjoyed her time with Lillian as they each worked on their own sewing project. Lillian hoped to win the contest at the World's Fair. Lizzie's original intent was to get back home. Now—she didn't know.

Jeremiah smiled as he inspected his gift, running his thumb over the intricate engraved detailing.

"I'd noticed your other pocket watch was older and the glass had a small crack." Lizzie's voice trembled.

"Thank you for the very thoughtful gift." Jeremiah tipped her chin up to look at her. "If we were alone, I would kiss you."

Lizzie smiled. "I wish we were."

Jeremiah leaned closer. "Such talk from a lady."

His cheeks would turn red if he knew how deeply she longed to kiss him. "We'd best get going. Father said it's close to seven blocks to the fairgrounds."

"I wish we could walk barefooted," Lillian said.

If Lillian saw the future, she would faint. While she'd love to walk barefooted, or wear cute sandals and tennis shoes, Lillian would gasp at how revealing clothing had become. Lizzie chuckled envisioning Lillian dressed in bikini or short shorts, her hands scurrying to cover her exposed flesh. "It won't be so bad if we talk while we walk."

The walk to the fair turned out to not be bad at all, compared to all the exhibits they visited. Lizzie couldn't believe she actually got to see and touch the Liberty Bell. There were too many exhibits to visit in a day, or even a week.

For dinner, they promised to meet Lizzie's family at Jeremiah's aunt's restaurant. Lizzie's stomach grumbled as they headed to meet her family. She enjoyed looping her arms around his as they walk. It was old-fashioned and cute. She smiled at Lillian and Thomas walking the same way in front of them, Thomas' arm bent, and his elbow extended for Lillian to hold too.

"I wish Father could meet your parents," Lizzie said.

"So, do I." Jeremiah's breath expelled slowly. "But if your father doesn't approve of my position, he may not approve of my father being a miner."

Lizzie's lips pursed. Her grip on Jeremiah's arm tightened a fraction. "I promise I'll try to talk to him again and get him to see that it doesn't matter what type of work a person does as long as they're providing for their family."

Jeremiah snickered. "Your father expects more. I can tell by the way he looks at me."

"Well, I don't care what he thinks." Lizzie's nose jutted a fraction. "It's not like we've even discussed a future together, and if we did, it's nobody's business but ours."

When they arrived at the restaurant, Lizzie's parents and sisters were already seated at a table. Jeremiah and Thomas greeted her mother before shaking her father's hand. Then the boys pulled another table over so that they could all sit together. Mother insisted that Lizzie sit next to her so that she could show Lizzie a swatch of the fabric that she was having curtains made from.

Jeremiah held the seat out for Lizzie and scooted it in as she sat—a chivalrous act she silently enjoyed.

"Why don't you sit next to me, Jeremiah?" Father said before Jeremiah could take the seat next to Lizzie.

She exchanged a brief glance with Jeremiah before he did as her father instructed.

A waitress came to their table and took their order. Mother was about to pull out her sample of fabric when Jeremiah's aunt approached the table.

His aunt said hello to Jeremiah and introduced herself to Lizzie's parents before coming to hug Lizzie's neck. "You've got a mighty fine daughter," his aunt said. "I've enjoyed getting to spend some time with her the last couple of months."

Father's eyebrow arched as he looked quizzically at Lizzie.

She met his gaze. Part of her wanted to sink beneath the table, the obstinate part of her screamed, *I'm an adult and can do what I want to do.*

"I'm hopeful my daughter has set a good example," Father said.

"She's a pure delight." Jeremiah's aunt smiled. "I best be getting back to the kitchen to get your supper ready."

"Thank you," Father said. His attention turned to Jeremiah.

Lizzie held her breath a moment but realized there was nothing she could do and nowhere to hide. As her grandmother always said, "let the chips fall where they may." She would deal with that fallout later.

"Don't you just love this fabric?" Mother's voice broke through Lizzie's thoughts. "I'm going to have curtains made for the sitting room and maybe a couple pillows for the sofa."

Gasping, Lizzie grabbed the swatch from her mother's hand. "That's it.

A light cream background, with what reminded Lizzie of a paisley design. There were multiple shades of green swirling leaves with burgundy, orange and a mustard color flowers—a very outdated design. The fabric was thicker than the other fabrics she was using to make the quilt.

She smiled as she rubbed the fabric between her fingers. "I need a yard of this for the quilt."

"I guess we could stop back by the shop after dinner," Mother said.

"Thank you, Mother." Lizzie hugged her. "I can't wait to get back home and start cutting out this fabric.

Then I'll only have one more fabric I need. Maybe they'll have that at the shop you got this from too?"

Mother's face looked downcast. "I'm afraid you'll have to wait awhile around six weeks."

Lizzie's eyes widened. "Six weeks?"

"I'm sorry, sweetie, and I have more bad news." Mother gently stroked Lizzie head with her hand. "The whole reason I went into that store was to look for the fabric you told me about, the one that woman's dress was made from. They didn't have it." Mother offered an apologetic smile. "Since we were already looking at fabric, I saw this one and decided to have curtains made."

"It's all right," Lizzie said. "If you hadn't of looked for me, you wouldn't have found this one. So, thank you."

"You're welcome, dear."

Mother was thoughtful, but Lizzie still couldn't get over the fact that it would take six weeks to get the fabric. That meant it wouldn't arrive until mid-August, and she still had to finish making the quilt which was taking longer than she expected.

Chapter Fifteen

Father had shown his disapproval upon returning from the family trip to the World's Fair. The most frustrating part was his refusal to discuss it on the way home. Then when he flat out refused to let her see Jeremiah again—like he somehow had control over what she did at her age—infuriated her. Which he also refused to talk about.

How did so many marriages survive in the 1900s if men had attitudes like this? Thankfully, Jeremiah listened and cared how she felt.

This week, she decided to make the best of her time at home at night by working on her quilt since she couldn't hang out with her friend. Lillian spent most of her evenings with Thomas. Lizzie wished she had the same opportunity with Jeremiah, but he lived in St. Louis and helped out at home. As strange as it was, she missed spending time with Lillian, or having the opportunity to go out on double-dates with her friend.

Lizzie skipped going to the train station twice that week to keep the peace in their home. Guilt niggled at her on the days that she did sneak off to the train depot to catch a couple minutes with Jeremiah before the train had to leave.

Friday, he'd told her he wished to speak with her father. She didn't know why. They didn't have long to discuss it, so she'd told him they would talk about it more on Sunday, after church. When she came home from the train station, she went in search of Mother.

Lizzie found her in the sitting room. "Mother?"

Mother looked up from the catalogue she was viewing. "Yes, dear?"

Butterflies danced in her stomach. If she couldn't talk to Father, perhaps Mother would be a go-between. Lizzie sat down on the settee next to Mother. "I'd like for Jeremiah to join us for lunch Sunday."

Mother's brown eyes looked weary. "I think it is too soon to approach Father on this."

"Don't you think it would be good for them to get to know each other?"

"I've already invited guests for lunch Sunday, and if you promise to do two things for me, I'll talk to your father about Jeremiah coming to dinner next Sunday. What do you say?" Mother asked.

Lizzie smiled. That sounded promising—a compromise. "Sure."

"Good." Mother returned her smile. "Mrs. Adams and her grandson are joining us for lunch. I would like for you to meet him and keep him company this week during his visit since he doesn't know anyone besides his grandmother."

"You want me to babysit?"

"No." Her mother laughed. "He's twenty-four, surely old enough to fend for himself."

"Then why do I have to keep him company?"

"So that he's not lonely and has a good time and wants to come back and see his grandmother more often." Mother frowned. "Who knows how many more years his grandmother has left. I don't think it is asking too much for you to help her out."

"Jeremiah is expecting me to go out with him Sunday, and we're going to be with Lillian and Thomas.

98

Not to mention, Monday is Jeremiah's day off." Lizzie stared at her hands in her lap. "Can't I wait to show her grandson around until Tuesday?"

"I think you already know the answer to that." Mother put her arm around Lizzie's shoulders. "Sunday's meal is the time for a proper introduction."

For months, Lizzie dreamed of getting back to her *real* life. It had taken her time to adjust to this era and what seemed like backwards ways at times. She'd learned things were more about formalities and proper etiquette. If she were back in her timeline, she could easily ignore her mother's request. Mainly because she didn't live at home. But here, now, she needed to make some concessions.

Lizzie nodded reluctantly.

Sunday morning, Lillian ran up to greet Lizzie outside of church when Lizzie's family arrived. Lillian beamed like a school girl, excited as ever. She must have had something she was dying to share.

"Hurry inside Lizzie." Mother gave Lizzie a *knowing* look. "Mrs. Adams and Henry will be sitting with us in church."

Lizzie nodded, and her parents continued heading into church, Mother holding each of the girls' hands.

"Henry?" Lillian's eyes widened. "Who's that?"

"He's Mrs. Adams grandson." Lizzie let out an exasperated sigh. "Mother made me agree to keep him company this week since he doesn't know anybody here, other than his grandmother. In exchange, she's willing to talk to Father about Jeremiah coming to lunch."

"How old is Henry?" A frown creased Lillian's brow.

"He a couple years older than you are." It was still hard for Lizzie to think of herself as only twenty-one, when she was twenty-eight in her real life. A life that seemed to be slipping further and further away.

"Jeremiah's not going to be happy because—" Lillian's eyes widened.

"Because what?"

Lillian's lips were pursed. Her eyes narrowed. "He's going to get the same impression that I am. Your parents are trying to arrange a match with you and Henry."

Lizzie chuckled. "That's silly."

"Oh, really?" Lillian rolled her eyes at Lizzie. "Says the girl who is going to ditch her beau this week to keep another man company."

"It's okay for people to be friends," Lizzie heard defensiveness in her own voice, but carried on, "it doesn't mean they're courting or dating. Whatever you all want to call it."

"Honestly, Lizzie, sometimes you act like you're not from around here."

It was Lizzie's turn for her lips to press together. She'd never told Lillian about her past life. Only Jeremiah knew the truth. She didn't want anyone else thinking she was crazy—like her family did the day she suddenly ended up in the past.

She shrugged. "I just think you're blowing things out of proportion and I hope you won't even suggest that my parents are fixing me up with Henry to Jeremiah. I don't need him upset with me when he has nothing to worry about."

"I won't say a word, but mind you Lizzie, you be careful because of your parents' intentions." Lillian hugged her. "I've always dreamed of me marrying Thomas and you marrying Jeremiah and us all being the best of friends for the rest of our lives."

Lizzie laughed, even though her head felt woozy. She'd never really thought about getting married. Besides, how could she? Her life was in the future.

"I need to go inside," she told Lillian. As she walked inside in a daze, Jeremiah's warm brown eyes and sweet smile haunted her thoughts. Being with Jeremiah would make her happy. He was undoubtedly the reason she hadn't been hard pressed to finish the quilt.

She found herself smiling as she slipped into the pew past her parents, not realizing until after she sat down that Olivia and Mary Margaret were seated between them, instead of on the other side of mother.

"This is Henry Adams," Mother said.

Lizzie turned to follow her gaze, realizing that she was seated next to him.

Henry looked slender and well dressed in an expensive pinstriped suit with a medium-blue bowtie that almost made Lizzie chuckle. He had blond hair and blue eyes. His chiseled jaw and dimple in his chin would have made most women swoon. But Lizzie wasn't most women.

"How do you do?" Henry smiled wide and took her hand in his, kissing the back of it. "I am pleased to make your acquaintance."

A giggle erupted. "I'm sorry." Lizzie's cheeks warmed. She didn't dare explain that she was laughing about the way he kissed her hand. Hopefully he didn't mistake it for infatuation. She'd seen Lillian do that all the time when she first started seeing Thomas. "My name's Lizzie."

After service, Lizzie noticed that Jeremiah approached Father instead of her. Lizzie assumed Lillian had already told Jeremiah that she had to spend the day with her family. Jeremiah probably noticed Henry and his grandmother. It wouldn't have escaped her attention if Jeremiah had been sitting with another woman in church. Even though there was nothing for him to worry about, he would have wanted to know what was going on. Lillian undoubtedly told him that Mrs. Adams and her grandson would be joining Lizzie's family for lunch. Maybe he wanted to see if Father would allow him to spend the day with them?

While their conversation was relatively short, the minutes dragged by slowly, putting Lizzie on edge. When their conversation ended, Jeremiah briskly turned and walked away, not even bothering to look in Lizzie's direction.

She hurried to speak with Father. "What did Jeremiah want? He looked upset."

"He asked a question and didn't get the answer he was hoping for," Father said. "He'll be fine."

"Is that all?" Lizzie wished she had the opportunity to speak with Jeremiah. Texting was one modern convenience she wished were available right now.

"That's all." Father's tone was clipped. "Besides, we need to get back to our guests."

One week, Lizzie reminded herself. That was Mother's requirement for Lizzie to get what she wanted. Given Father's mood and conversation with Jeremiah a few moments ago, she didn't dare broach the topic with him.

Chapter Sixteen

After lunch, Lizzie persuaded Henry to go for a walk. She failed to include her ulterior motives, deciding it best in case Henry happened to mention to her family that they ran into some of Lizzie's friends on their walk.

Several times Henry had reached toward her, or for her elbow, and Lizzie had carefully moved another step away.

"Are you seeing anyone special back home?" Lizzie asked.

"I wondered if you were nervous." Henry laughed. "Turns out you were merely jealous, which you needn't be." Henry smiled.

He was charming, but he wasn't Jeremiah. "Actually, if we're being honest, I have feeling for someone and I'm afraid he may be upset that I'm spending the day with you."

"I don't blame him," Henry said. "If you were my girl, I wouldn't want to share you with anyone else either."

Lizzie's cheeks warmed. "My mother told me I had to keep you company this week if I wanted to have him over for lunch next Sunday."

Henry nodded, absorbing her words much better than Lizzie expected. "So, what you're telling me is, I don't have a chance of winning your heart?"

Smiling at his words, Lizzie gently laid a hand on his bicep. "I'm sorry. You're very sweet, but I don't have feelings for you."

He stopped on the sidewalk, and she did too, turning to look at him. Henry brushed a stray hair from her face. "This man that you care for is very lucky. I find your beautiful brown eyes entrancing and could easily get lost in their depths."

"You're making me blush." Lizzie knew her cheeks had to be warm. "I know it is a lot to ask, but would you mind if we went by his friend's house to see if he is there?" Lizzie sighed. "I feel bad that I didn't get to talk to him at church this morning and don't want him to be upset."

"I'd be happy to meet the young gentleman who stole your heart."

She searched Henry's face for any signs of sarcasm, and only saw sincerity in his eyes and the warmth of his charming smile. "Thank you."

"For what?" His left eye squinted as he looked at her quizzically.

"For being kind and understanding of my predicament." Lizzie gave him a brief hug. "You're a true gentleman."

"My pleasure," he said. "But I must admit I am curious about the man who beat me out."

Lizzie laughed. "The heart wants what the heart wants."

"Such wise words from such a beautiful lady." He looked around. "Which direction do we head to see your beau?"

Lizzie pointed. "We need to make a right at the corner and it's halfway down the block."

"So, we're close?"

"Yes."

He laughed. "I take it we were already headed in this direction to see him?"

"I'm sorry." She felt a little guilty admitting it. "But it was bothering me all through lunch."

"Come on." Henry took her hand and headed down the street.

They were nearly to Thomas' home before Lizzie realized she was still holding Henry's hand, and tighter than she should have. She released it under the pretense of straightening the fabric of her dress before climbing the steps leading to his front door. Taking a deep breath, she knocked as she slowly expelled the air from her lungs.

Henry waited at the bottom of the stairs, leaning casually against the railing while they waited for someone to answer the door.

Hearing footsteps, Lizzie's heart began to race.

After a few moments, Thomas opened the door. He didn't look excited to see her, and his response for Henry was a scowl.

Lizzie swallowed the lump in her throat. "Can I please speak with Jeremiah?"

"He's not here."

Her eyes widened. "What do you mean, he's not here?"

Lillian came to the door, holding a wrapped package and an envelope. "Jeremiah left this for you."

"Thank you." She took the items from Lillian. "But where did he go?"

Thomas glanced at Henry, and then back at her. "I assume he went back home."

"He didn't have any reason to be jealous." Lizzie assumed that was why he left. "Can I talk to you—" Lizzie chanced a glance at Thomas before turning her attention back to Lillian, "privately?"

Thomas retreated into the other room and Lillian stepped outside. As she and Lizzie took a seat on the steps, Lizzie asked Henry to please give them some privacy. He nodded, smiled at Lillian, and casually strolled a safe distance away, admiring the surroundings as he hummed.

Lizzie thought it was sweet of him to oblige. Not the most exciting day of his vacation. She would have to make it up to him.

"Please tell me Jeremiah wasn't jealous," Lizzie sighed. "Is that why he left?"

"No, Lizzie, that's not why he left exactly."

"What do you mean?" Lizzie rubbed her temple. She was getting a headache and her stomach churned.

Tears welled in Lillian's eyes. "Oh, Lizzie, he was going to ask you to marry him."

Lizzie's jaw dropped. She stared at Lillian. Her heart stopped, so did her breathing. This must have been what suspended animation felt like.

"Jeremiah wanted to propose?" Lizzie's voice sounded like a whisper in her own ears. Her words slowly penetrated her thought pattern. Her eyes widened. "He doesn't now?" The beating of her heart accelerated. "Was it because he saw me sitting next to Henry?"

"No, Lizzie." Lillian's eyes held deep sorrow. "After church, he asked your father for permission and he said no."

"He what?" Lizzie's fist clenched, and she clutched the package closer to her chest. "We don't need Father's permission to get married."

"Your father won't pay for the wedding," Lillian said.

"We can always elope." Without having time to realize what her reaction would have been to Jeremiah's proposal, her heart had already made the decision for her—even if her head would have argued against staying in the past forever. She couldn't imagine Jeremiah not being a part of her life. "Do you know if Jeremiah will be back tomorrow?"

"I don't think so."

"Please tell Jeremiah that I need to speak to him in person."

Lillian looked at the package in Lizzie's hands. "You might want to read his letter."

"Why?" Lizzie didn't like the sound of Lillian's voice.

"Let's sit down on the step, Lizzie," Lillian said, taking her arm to turn her around.

They sat down.

Lizzie laid the package across her lap and held her breath as she began to open the envelope containing Jeremiah's letter. Her hands shook. She took the paper out and unfolded it carefully.

Dear Lizzie,

My heart is heavier now than I could ever begin to convey. When I came to church today, I had intended to ask your father to marry you.

I believed that I could convince him how much we were in love. However, he informed me that they had introduced you to someone whom he believed you were better suited for, and that if I loved you as I claimed, I would want the very best for you. I tried to assure him that I believed that you needed me as much as I needed you. He then informed me that he would never give his blessing for us to marry, and that if I continued to try seeing you, he would do everything in his power to see that I never worked for the railroad company again.

My family counts on my income to help them get by, and without this job, I would not be able to afford to support a wife. So, it is with deep regret that I am going away.

I was able to find the fabric that you needed for your quilt. I had debated on giving it to you because I couldn't bear the thought of your dream being true—and you going away. But now, I truly hope that you are able to go back home. I want you to be happy and pray that one day you will find someone in your future—wherever that future turns out being.

All my love,
Jeremiah

"What's wrong?" Henry's voice drew her attention away from the letter. "Why are you crying?"

Lizzie wanted to lash out at him, but it wasn't Henry's fault. "I'm afraid I won't be able to keep you company this week."

"Is it because your beau was jealous?" Concern shown in Henry's eyes.

"No." She shook her head. "He wanted to marry me, and Father wouldn't give his blessing. In fact, he threatened him."

"I'm sorry, Lizzie." He thrust his hands into his trouser pockets. "I wish I could hug you, or comfort you somehow. I hate to see you cry."

"I have a feeling I'll be doing a lot of it for a very long while."

Chapter Seventeen

"I hate you and I never want to speak to you again," Lizzie spewed the words out like venom as soon as she walked through the door and stomped to her room. Tossing the gift from Jeremiah on the bed, she sat down and swiped at a tear she felt rolling down her cheek. Opening the envelope, she took out Jeremiah's letter and read it again.

Mother opened Lizzie's door.

Anger welled up in Lizzie as her hands tightened on the letter. "You lied to me."

"Elizabeth Ruth Ambrewster."

"Peterson, my last name is Peterson," Lizzie corrected her in a low, gravelly voice. Right now, she didn't want to be their daughter, or even their great-great-great-granddaughter. Jeremiah was the only one holding her here—to this life. If she couldn't have him, she wanted to go home—to her real home. "I can't believe you had the audacity to tell me you were going to ask your husband to allow Jeremiah to come for lunch next Sunday, and all along you knew he was going to tell Jeremiah he wasn't welcome."

Mother's mouth opened in what Lizzie assumed was surprise, or perhaps she was astounded at Lizzie's outburst.

Maybe she didn't know, but it didn't matter, and it certainly didn't change the situation.

Lizzie wanted to fix things between her and Jeremiah. But how? Cell phones hadn't been invented yet, and not every home even had a regular phone. Jeremiah's didn't. To make matters worse, Lizzie didn't have a car, so she couldn't just pick up and go see if he'd gone home.

"I gave you my word," Mother said. "I fully intended to talk to your father. But it appears you are the one not keeping up your end of the bargain. Poor Henry looks upset. He insisted that his grandmother leave with him immediately."

"Good." At least someone had the decency to show some decorum. "You should have never tried to play matchmaker. You knew how I felt about Jeremiah."

Mother sighed and moved closer. "May I sit down?"

Lizzie scooted over to make room.

Taking a seat, Mother turned and reached a hand out toward Lizzie, but Lizzie moved, and Mother settled for folding her hands in her lap. "Please tell me what happened after you left? What made you so upset?"

Her throat felt constricted. Instead of telling Mother, Lizzie handed her the letter.

"What dream?" Mother asked. "Were you planning to run away? Or did he think your father would ask you to leave home if you went against his wishes?" Mother's eyes were wide and intense as she stared at Lizzie.

"You wouldn't understand." Which was true. When Lizzie woke that morning back in April, Father threatened to have her committed. Telling either of them the truth wasn't an option. She needed to find a job, in case she couldn't get back home. After what Father did, she had no intention of staying in his house any longer than she had to be there. "I need to finish my quilt."

Mother nodded and walked to the door. Pausing, she turned around and looked at Lizzie, her eyes filled with concern. "You know your father only wants what's best for you."

"Then why did he threaten Jeremiah?"

Mother didn't have an answer for her question.

"Tell me this, did your parents force you to marry Father against your will, or were you truly in love with him?"

"I was in love with him," Mother said. "We married when we were teenagers."

"And it had nothing to do with his education or his job?" Lizzie asked.

She shook her head in response to Lizzie's question.

"Then if you were both allowed to choose each other, why do you insist on interfering in my life? Shouldn't I be able to choose who I want to marry too?"

"I'm sorry, Lizzie." Mother closed her eyes a moment and sighed. "I promise to talk about the situation with Father tonight."

Lizzie stayed up until the wee hours of the morning working on the quilt. She still needed the fabric from Mother's curtains, which wouldn't be delivered for another four to six weeks. As the night wore on, her mind became number, clouded with decisions until sleep overtook her. By the time she woke, she realized it was too late to make it to the train station to catch a ride to St. Louis.

After dressing, Lizzie wandered into the dining room, intent on finding something to eat. Father was seated at the table. Normally, he would have already left for work. She averted her gaze, darting toward the kitchen.

"Lizzie," Father said. "I know you're upset but hear me out."

She stopped, fists clenched at her sides.

"Unless you plan to tell me you were wrong, and you insist on driving me to St. Louis so that you can apologize to Jeremiah, then I have nothing to say to you."

"If that's what it will take," Father said, "Get yourself something to eat and we'll leave in the next half hour."

Lizzie's mouth dropped. "You're serious?"

Father nodded. "I'm sorry, Lizzie. I shouldn't have interfered. Your mother was right, Jeremiah is a good man, and with the love of a good woman by his side, a good man can do anything."

She almost ran to hug him but reminded herself that his actions were the reason she was in this situation to begin with. "I'll be ready."

What should have taken less than four hours to drive, took closer to six because they didn't have the interstates and faster speed to travel. The first hour-and-a-half, Lizzie worked on her quilt until sleepiness overtook her and she dosed off until Father woke her for directions in the city.

By the time they arrived at Jeremiah's house, her heart beat faster than the tune to The Little Drummer Boy.

"Wait here," Lizzie said. "I'll go talk to him first."

Lizzie tucked strands of her long brown hair behind her ear, silently wishing she'd had time to make herself more presentable.

Jeremiah's parents' home was a fourth the size of the house she lived in now. Lizzie had been inside, and even upstairs to where the two small bedrooms and an equally tiny area between the rooms that served as Jeremiah's bedroom. To her, they were *tiny houses* before their time, or maybe they had just become popular again in the future. She climbed the stairs to the older, home and knocked on the grayish-blue wooden door.

The minutes ticked by slowly before Jeremiah's younger brother, Nehemiah, answered the door. "Lizzie?"

Nehemiah looked a lot like Jeremiah, except his face was fuller and he was an inch shorter. It was obvious he was surprised to see her by his stunned silence and dropped-jaw.

The surprise on Nehemiah's face concerned Lizzie. "Can I speak with Jeremiah?"

"He's gone, Lizzie." Nehemiah's Adam's apple bobbed as he swallowed. "He took a train last night and said he took on a longer run. He said wouldn't be able to make it home for a long while but would send money to help out."

Air whooshed out of Lizzie's lung, making her chest tighten. "He didn't tell you which route he was going to be working on?"

"No."

"I've got to speak with him, Nehemiah." Lizzie took a step closer to Jeremiah's brother, her eyes boring into his. "Father's had a change of heart. He even came to apologize."

Nehemiah looked past Lizzie, to where Father was waiting in the car. "I don't know what to say, Lizzie." Nehemiah's eyes softened as he met her gaze. "I promise I'll tell him as soon as we hear from him, but he was pretty upset when he left. It may be a while before I can get word to him."

A tear trickled down her cheek.

"Don't lose heart, Lizzie." Nehemiah squeezed her shoulders gently. "Jeremiah will be so excited to hear the news. He loves you and he'll wait for you. I'm sure of it."

Chapter Eighteen

Warrensburg, Missouri — December 1904

The days ticked by into weeks, and even months with no word from Jeremiah. Summer had passed, and winter was fast approaching.

Mother's curtains and the fabric Lizzie needed to finish the quilt had arrived much later than expected because of all the orders that had been sold at the World's Fair. Lizzie had even visited the fair before Thanksgiving, hoping maybe Jeremiah's aunt would have seen or heard from him. Nehemiah told her that his brother continued to send money home but hadn't been in touch. He'd asked some of the other men who worked the rail to relay a message to Jeremiah if they saw him.

Lizzie's heart was torn between holding out hope to see Jeremiah again, or praying to go home if they couldn't be together. Each stitch she sewed brought her closer to having to make a decision of how she wanted to spend her future. She couldn't bear the thought of being stuck in the past without Jeremiah.

"Lizzie, Lizzie," Mary Margaret and Olivia's squeals sounded through the house before they came bursting into her bedroom.

She saw Mother coming down the hall through the open door. Lizzie put the needle into a pin cushion and set her quilt aside.

"What's wrong?" she asked Mother as she walked into the room.

"There's a letter, Lizzie." Mother held out an envelope for her to take. "Your young man has finally written."

"He what?" Lizzie stammered, taking the letter in her trembling hand. She opened it and began to read.

Dear Lizzie,

Please forgive me for leaving so abruptly in July. After speaking with your father, I was heartbroken that he refused to give his blessing. I have just received news that your father changed his mind and is willing to allow me to court you.

I have talked to my boss and they will let me go back to my old route on the railroad in another week or two. You don't know how much I worried that you'd finished your quilt and gone away. Please give me a chance to make up for the heartache my absence has caused you. I expect to be home before Christmas and look forward to seeing you.

All my love,
Jeremiah

"He's coming home." Lizzie smiled and clutched the letter to her chest. "He'll be here before Christmas."

"That's wonderful news, Lizzie," Mother said.

"Yeah," Mary Margaret squealed.

Olivia's eyes widened. "Is he bringing us presents for Christmas?"

It was funny the way children's minds worked. Lizzie laughed. "I think his coming home is the best gift we could ask for."

Lizzie knew what gift she would give Jeremiah for Christmas—she'd give him the quilt, a sign that she would rather stay here with him. Her heart flooded with warmth. She'd finish it tonight before bed.

Warrensburg, Missouri – December 17, 1904

Saturday afternoon, Lizzie draped the crazy quilt across her bed so that she could admire her work while she wrapped Christmas presents. It had taken her many months to find and retrieve the fabrics needed for the quilt and to hand stitch it together. She felt a sense of accomplishment but was even more excited to be giving the quilt away to Jeremiah.

If you had told her back in April that she would want to stay here, she would have thought it a cruel joke. While she missed her family, her time here with Jeremiah had helped her heart to mend. Geoff's betrayal no longer mattered, because he didn't matter. Lizzie had managed to find love again, in the strangest place—the past.

Lizzie smiled as she laid the adorable curly brunette-haired rag doll on the red wrapping paper and folded the sides over, before taping them together.

A heavy knock sounded on her bedroom door. Her heart raced. "Mary Margaret or Olivia, if either of you open that door you're not going to get any presents come Christmas morning."

Mother had promised to keep them busy while Lizzie wrapped their presents. The girls were as excited as any child who'd just been told they were having a snow day. They could hardly be contained.

"Lizzie, it's me," Mother said. "Someone is here to see you."

Jeremiah?

"I'll be right there." She hurried and finished taping the wrapping paper so that Olivia wouldn't be able to sneak a peek while Lizzie was visiting. Her heart raced. Jeremiah had said he'd be back before Christmas. Lizzie was beginning to wonder how much longer he was going to make her wait.

Lizzie stopped in front of the mirror and ran her brush through her hair, adding a fresh coat of lipstick before rubbing her lips together. It had been so long since she'd shared a kiss with Jeremiah. She wondered if Mother would gasp if she kissed him in front of her. She giggled at the thought and smiled even wider at her reflection before smoothing the long layers of her green dress.

Opening the door, she practically scurried down the hall to the sitting room. She stopped short. "Thomas? Where's Jeremiah?"

His face was downcast. When he looked up, she noticed he'd been crying.

Air whooshed from her lungs. "What's wrong?"

"There's been an accident, Lizzie," Thomas said. "The train derailed. Twenty-nine people were killed and numerous were injured."

"Jeremiah was injured?" Lizzie's words were barely a whisper.

Thomas shook his head. A tear rolled down his cheek. "No, Lizzie, he's…"

"Dead?" She shook her head. "No, it can't be…it can't be." The room began to swirl.

Father caught her as her body slumped. "Let me help you to the settee."

118

Lizzie sat there numb, leaning on the arm of the seat. Tears trickled down her cheeks.

"He was on his way back," Thomas said, "coming to see you."

A chill ran up her spine. Did Jeremiah die because of her?

"I don't feel well." Lizzie rubbed her arms and laid her head against the arm of the settee, curling her legs up. Numbness overtook her as she stared blankly, still unable to comprehend Jeremiah's death. "I just can't—"

She felt so cold but couldn't move.

Her mind tried to formulate images of her time with Jeremiah. Lizzie hadn't seen him since July. Hope had given her something to hold onto—a reason to stay connected to her surroundings, but now…

The weight coupled with a sense of warmth drew her attention as she realized Father had covered her up. It took a moment more for the pattern of the quilt to register. He'd taken the quilt off of her bed. Fresh tears streamed down her face as she drew the quilt up over her shoulder, burying herself beneath its warmth. Jeremiah would have liked her gift, but now that he wasn't coming back, it served only to remind her off her loss.

Chapter Nineteen

Warrensburg, Missouri – Present Day

Daylight streaming through the window made Lizzie squint. Her emotions were spent. She'd apparently fallen asleep on the settee. Lizzie stretched. Her eyes flew open. She shot up into a sitting position and looked around. The quilt was still covering her, but she wasn't in the sitting room any more.

"Grandma Mullane? Grandma Bader?" Lizzie hopped out of bed and ran to the living room.

"What's wrong, dear?" Grandma Mullane asked.

They were both watching TV.

"You're both here." Lizzie blinked several times.

"Of course, we're here." Grandma Bader glanced at her. "Don't worry about lunch. I made us soup and sandwiches."

"Lunch?" Lizzie was confused.

"Yes, you were going to make us something to eat before you had to go to the train station." Grandma Bader looked at the cuckoo clock on the wall above the television. She paused her show and set the remote down on the coffee table. "Your train will be leaving in a little over an hour. Why don't you sit down and talk for a few minutes? You look a little pale and your eyes are puffy, like you were crying."

"I was," Lizzie admitted as she took a seat in the leather, cream wingback chair. "It seemed so real."

"Oh, my." Grandma Mullane nudged Grandma Bader and pointed at Lizzie. "She looks like she's about to cry."

Lizzie wiped at the rebellious tear as it trickled down her cheek. "I'm fine."

"Maybe you'd feel better if you told us about your dream," Grandma Mullane suggested.

"You'll think this weird, but I actually dreamed about Great-great-grandma Ambrewster." She laughed, even though it wasn't funny. "That I was back in 1904 and I had the make the quilt in order to get back home."

"Obviously you did since you're here." Grandma Bader chuckled. "Ambrewster was her maiden name. She went on to marry Charles Lillingston."

Lizzie had forgotten what Grandma Mullane's maiden name was. At least her great-great grandmother had been able to move on. Lizzie decided not to go into too much detail about her dream. She didn't want to relive Jeremiah's death. The loss felt so real.

She did enjoy spending time with the little girls in her dream. "Her two younger sisters, Olivia and Mary Margaret were adorable."

"How did you know about my aunts?" Great-grandma Mullane asked. "I must have mentioned my mother's sisters before."

Lizzie's eyes widened. Maybe she had. She really couldn't remember.

"We best let Lizzie get ready, Mother, or she'll miss her train." Grandma Mullane stood. "I've got a book I promised to let your mother read if you don't mind taking it to her for me."

"I'd be happy to." Lizzie followed her grandmother to the other room to retrieve the book, before going to pack the rest of her things in her duffel bag and grabbing her quilt.

Heaviness weighed heavily on her heart as she said her goodbyes and went to the train station. The stone building was an older version of the past. Had her mind conjured a cleaner, newer version of the depot? Did she only have the dream because of her grandmother giving her the quilt?

By far the most vivid dream she ever had in her life. Whatever the reason for the dream, Lizzie felt she had finally moved past her hurt and was able to open her heart again, just as her great-great-grandmother was finally able to do as well. So, if Grandma Mullane had intended for her mother's story to help Lizzie get over Geoff—it worked.

"All aboard," announced over a speaker in the train station drew Lizzie's attention. She hurried outside with her things, ticket in hand, and climbed the few steps to board the train.

As she walked down the narrow aisle, her gaze locked with an incredible pair of brown eyes. "Jeremiah?"

"I'm sorry. Do I know you?" he asked.

Lizzie smiled. "You used to."

"That sounds like a story I need to hear." His laughter echoed in her ears. "Perhaps you would like to join me, and you could tell me your name and how you know me." He stood and allowed her room to pass him to sit at the window seat. "Please tell me you're not a social media stalker."

She giggled nervously. "Um, no. I promise, but you might find it kind of weird."

"Well, I've got three or four hours to kill before the train reaches St. Louis."

Tiny bursts of electricity tingled through her body. "I live in St. Louis too."

"You don't say." His left eyebrow arched slightly, and his smile melted her heart. "I'm afraid I don't know what to call you, other than beautiful."

Heat rose to her cheeks. "My name's Lizzie."

"Obviously, you already know my name is Jeremiah." He took her hand as if to shake it, but just held it. "So where have we met before? The train?"

Lizzie smiled. He'd never believe her if she told him. Although, he had believed her in her dream. She rubbed her hand over the quilt, tracing the flower patterns with her index finger. "Do you see the navy-blue centers of these flowers?"

He nodded when she glanced at him.

"They were from a torn pair of work pants that Jeremiah Hopkins wore when he worked on the train."

"Wait a minute." His eyes scrunched as lips twisted. "You're saying that fabric came from my namesake, my great-great uncle?"

"Yes," Lizzie said. "My great-great grandmother was in love with him and had planned to marry him."

"You're Elizabeth Ambrewster?" Jeremiah stared at her in disbelief. "We were just talking about her and how my great-grandfather spoke of how he went away when he thought her father wouldn't let them marry."

"You were talking about me? I mean her," Lizzie corrected herself, still feeling disorientated by her dream.

"Well, I was named after him, so it's a story that's kind of passed down over the years." Jeremiah ran his hand through his wavy brown hair. It was shorter on the sides than his great-great grandfather's.

Lizzie longed to reach out and touch it. Time was surreal. It seemed like months since she'd seen him, touched him, yet she'd only just woken from her nap over an hour ago.

Over the next few hours they shared stories of each other's families and talked as if they'd known each other their whole lives and were just catching up over 'old times'.

"Our stop is coming soon," Jeremiah said, brushing a strand of hair from her face. The action sending a surge of warmth through her. "Do you think we could maybe have dinner sometime? I'd love for you to meet my family."

His family? As odd as it sounded, it made sense. Their families were connected in a strange sense, and perhaps this was the time for their story. But the sense of loss still weighed heavily on her.

"I will, on one condition," Lizzie said.

"Now you really have me curious." Jeremiah leaned closer. His breath was warm against her ear. "What's your one condition?"

"We can't have history repeating itself," Lizzie breath was ragged. "Promise me you'll never ride the train again."

"For the mere price of a kiss, and dinner of course," he added, "I promise I'll never ride the train again. After all, I'd much prefer a long car ride alone with you, where we can hold hands without two little girls watching."

Her heart pounded. Lizzie turned to look in the direction he was motioning with his head. She laughed, realizing she half-expected Olivia and Mary Margaret to be seated behind them.

"Let's give them something to giggle about." Jeremiah used his index finger to gently turn her head back around to him. He leaned even closer, his lips claiming hers in a kiss that promised to erase the past and fill her future with hope, love, and possibilities.

The only thing Lizzie knew for sure was, as soon as she got home, she was going to lock her great-great grandmother's quilt away in the trunk at the foot of her bed and hide the key so that no one was ever tempted to pull the quilt out and use it again. She had no intention of going anywhere again—she was right where she wanted to be, and with the person she wanted to be with—through all of time.

Dear Reader,

Have you ever wondered what it would be like to have lived over a hundred years ago? Lizzie had the unexpected chance to find out. She also had a chance to learn that life goes on after heartache, and you can still find happiness in your future if you open yourself up and let others in.

While I was doing research for this story, I learned several things about the 1904 World's Fair, and my hometown. Did you know iced tea and waffle cones were believed to have been invented at the World's Fair? I also found out one country represented there was supplied dogs... to eat! Even if we prefer to keep dogs and cats as pets, and not food sources, the World's Fair gave people the chance to experience different cultures.

The 1904 World's Fair Flight Cage later became the cornerstone for the St. Louis Zoo. I think of all the treasures our city has because of the planning that went into such a magnificent event. If you ever visit St. Louis, you should make time to visit our zoo where you can still see the walk-through bird cage from the 1904 World's Fair.

Thank you for taking the time to read A Stitch in Time.

Blessings,

Susette
(Go to the next page to read an excerpt of Little Orphan Annie.)

Little Orphan Annie

By Susette Williams

CHAPTER ONE

"We've got a problem. Annie found out she was adopted." Roger Spelman sounded nervous as he relayed the information to the man who had *handled* their adoption.

"So? I'm assuming you made up a story?" He clutched the phone in one hand and rubbed the top of his head with the other, while he waited for Roger to respond. Over the years, his hair had thinned. He was getting too old to dodge obstacles. Most ties to his past had been severed and he'd started over fresh. Apparently, he'd left a few loose ends and by the sound of it, they were starting to unravel.

"Of course, I did. I told her that her biological parents were killed in a car accident." Roger paused. "She wants to find out if she has any distant relatives. I told her if she did have family left, she would have gone to them instead of being put up for adoption, but she insists on looking anyway."

"Then it appears you have a problem. We can't have her snooping around, asking questions about the agency or her biological family."

"But you closed the agency," Roger insisted. "I'm sure she won't get far in her pursuit. I just thought you should know."

"I'm glad you told me." That way he could take care of something before it became a problem, namely a nosey little girl. "But Roger..."

"Yes?"

"If she gets too close, we will have to eliminate the threat." He leaned forward in his chair, his fingers drummed methodically on the desk as he contemplated how to alleviate his problem. The last thing he wanted was to spend his retirement in prison.

"You wouldn't?" Roger's voice quivered.

It didn't do for anyone to underestimate him. "I would."

* * *

Annie Spelman tapped her French manicured nails along the rim of the steering wheel of her rental car while she waited for Child Rescue to open. She'd called numerous other agencies for help, and two of them had suggested she try this place. From what she'd been able to gather on her own, the adoption agency had been in Missouri, but there didn't appear to be any current information on them. Coming here seemed the most logical choice, and she wasn't about to let someone hang up on her or tell them they couldn't help her. If need be, she'd guilt them with the fact that she'd had to fly here and rent a car just to make sure she could talk to somebody. They had to help her.

Another glance at her watch revealed five minutes remained. She felt like a kid waiting for the toy store to open.

She enjoyed the gentle breeze blowing through her open window. Back home, in the part of California she lived in, mornings were usually chilly. Not like the afternoon when you sought the comfort of an air conditioner. When she arrived at the hotel last night, she'd wanted to go for a walk and waited for the evening to cool down—but it never did. The weather in Missouri was different than back home. If she'd come in the winter, instead of the fall, she could have at least seen some snow. She'd only seen snow when she went on a ski trip her senior year.

A red Avenger pulled up in front of her and all thoughts about the weather and growing humidity faded away. The driver's side door opened and a tall, handsome man, with shoulders that looked broad enough to carry the weight of the world, climbed out of the car. While his stride exuded an air of self-confidence, his frown belied a hint of weariness. He ran a hand through his rumpled brown hair as he headed around to the passenger's side and opened the door for the other person.

Annie wondered if they were a couple who'd lost a child, until a woman well beyond childbearing years, wielding an attitude and sporting a cane between gnarled white fingers, climbed out of the vehicle. When he tried to help the woman, she pushed him away. As the woman lifted her cane and jabbed it toward the man in an attempt to get him to leave her alone, Annie giggled.

"I don't need any help," the woman said in a loud crackly voice.

Thoughts of her own grandmother melted Annie's heart. The anniversary of her grandmother's death would be in a few weeks, nearly a month before Annie's twenty-fifth birthday. Her grandmother had been a very determined person, as well. She understood how the woman felt. When you spent your life nurturing your family you didn't expect people to start taking care of you one day.

She sighed. Would she ever find any of her real family? Losing the woman, she knew as Grandmother had shattered her world, even more than when she found out she was adopted. But in the midst of disappointment and hurt, she had hope. While her adoptive father said her birth parents had been killed in a car accident, there existed the slightest possibility that she may have a grandparent or other family member, even a distant relative still living. The fact that her adoptive father didn't want her to pursue her biological family troubled Annie. Perhaps that's why he never told her of her adoption—to keep her from looking. Whatever the reason, it didn't matter now. In a few short minutes, the agency would open, and she'd be able to enlist their help to find her family.

She glanced at her watch. Two minutes to go. The people who'd climbed out of the Avenger were going to have to wait along with her.

The man fidgeted with his keys. He inserted one into the door, opened the agency and went inside. He continued to hold the door for his older companion. Apparently, they didn't have to wait.

Annie fumbled for her door handle. Grabbing her purse, she jumped out of her Lexus. She bolted for the agency.

The man started to close the door, but Annie pushed against it with more force than necessary.

"Whoa." The man staggered backward and bumped into a desk. "What's the hurry, Slick? There aren't any sales going on in here."

"Sales?" He didn't make sense. Neither did the fact that she couldn't help but stare into his unbelievably blue eyes. "You lost me." And so did his eyes. The color was almost hypnotic, like a rare gemstone.

He laughed. "You came barging in here like there was a Black Friday sale going on."

"Oh, I'm sorry." Annie blinked. Her cheeks warmed. "The secretary wouldn't let me in earlier."

"That's because we're not open." Mr. Wonderful smiled, revealing his pearly whites.

Annie found herself smiling, too.

"You are open, Ian." The older woman tapped the watch on her wrist. "So, shouldn't you get to work? The woman obviously came here because she needed help, not directions to the mall." The woman winked at Annie, then meandered down the hall with her cane.

"My grandmother's right. I'm sorry." A muscle in Ian's jaw twitched. "Why don't you give me a few minutes to get situated, and then we can talk."

"Thanks." Annie sat in one of the chairs Ian gestured toward.

Annie's heart raced. She dismissed the thought that it may have something to do with Ian and chalked it up to the excitement of finding her real family.

* * *

Ian shook his head and took a deep breath, which he slowly expelled as he walked into his office. Grandma had already taken her seat at the makeshift desk near his and booted up the computer. He shouldn't have taught her how to play Spider Solitaire. She complained and talked to the computer as if it could hear her.

"I'm going to beat your score today," she said over her shoulder.

Ian doubted it. He'd beat the easy level in ninety-one moves. His grandmother hadn't won in less than a hundred and twenty. He smiled. When he was a kid, Grandma would let him win games to encourage him. He wondered if she regretted that now. "I'm going to be interviewing a client in a few minutes, Grandma. Can you promise to be good?"

"I'm always good, my boy." Grandma's mischievous smile contradicted her claims.

What could he do? Grandma had run off several women he'd hired to help her. Maybe he should look for a young, handsome man who would keep her mind off of being obstinate. Who was he kidding? Handsome men didn't take jobs as caregivers to aging clients, especially if the clients didn't have money.

Ian sighed as he sat behind his desk. He picked up the phone. "Jan, if you haven't already, would you have our guest fill out a new client form, and give me at least ten minutes before you send her in? Thanks."

He couldn't believe he hadn't even taken the time to introduce himself to the woman. It wasn't like him. He couldn't afford to lose business by being inconsiderate. If he didn't find someone to help with his grandmother soon, he'd be sunk.

Ian opened the folder on his desk. A picture of Jeremy stared back at him. *I'll find your killer,* Ian promised himself. He was close. Tracking fugitives on the run proved an interesting challenge, but he experienced more satisfaction when he found a missing child and reunited the family.

One case in particular haunted him. If it hadn't been for Janie Lohman's disappearance, he would have never gotten involved in this business or started his own agency. As each day passed, hopes of finding her dimmed. Too many other cases demanded his immediate attention. He wouldn't finish the case he was on before another client walked through the door. He had little time to dedicate to looking for his neighbor's daughter. Having to play babysitter to his grandmother didn't help matters either. Guilt washed over Ian. He shouldn't ponder selfish thoughts. If it weren't for his grandmother, he wouldn't have had anywhere to go when his parents died. He loved his grandmother like a mother.

The clicking of the office door handle brought Ian back to the present. He closed Jeremy's folder and put it aside, then stood. "Please come in and have a seat."

"Thank you." The woman handed him the clipboard in her hands. "Your secretary got a phone call. I told her I could find my way to your office."

Ian took the clipboard while offering his other hand for her to shake. "Thank you. I hope you don't mind that my grandmother is keeping me company at work today."

"No, that's fine." Annie's smile looked genuine.

With formalities out of the way, he glanced down at the form as they both took their seats. He continued to read. She hadn't filled in the name of her husband. Maybe they were separated due to the loss of their child. "Will your husband be joining us?"

"I'm not married," Annie said.

"Wait a minute." Ian paused as he reread the form. "Your parents are the missing persons?" Ian looked up and saw quizzical brown eyes staring at him.

"Yes."

Grandma laughed.

Ian wanted to reach over and nudge her into silence.

"We find missing children," Ian said. "That's why our agency is called Child Rescue."

"I know." Annie sighed. "But I've tried everywhere I can think of to find the adoption agency my parents went through and haven't had any luck. My adoptive parents won't help. In fact, my father has practically disowned me because he's so angry that I insisted on pursuing this."

Was that a tear? It wrenched his gut to see a woman cry. Annie brushed her rosy cheeks with the side of her index finger.

"I require a five-thousand-dollar retainer." He didn't know what made him open his big mouth and encourage her. He didn't have time to take on her case. Especially if he'd have to take Grandma in tow everywhere he went. Once he found a caregiver for his grandmother, he could take on more cases. Until then—he was stuck.

"I don't know that I can spare that much." Annie's brown eyes glistened. She blinked rapidly a few times. She swallowed hard before going on. "I work for my father's company, but he won't allow me to work there if I continue to look for my real family."

"Why is your adoptive father against you finding your biological parents?" Ian thought it odd that they would go to such great lengths to keep her from looking for her family but held his tongue so as not to make her defensive.

"I don't know," Annie stammered. "He's jealous. I'm sure that's all it is. My parents weren't even the ones who told me about the adoption."

"How did you find out?" Ian asked.

"My cousin made a flippant comment while we were shopping. She said you'd never know I was adopted by the way I spend money." Annie blushed. "She was only teasing, but it slipped out. Apparently, she'd overheard her parents talking about it when she was little. They told her not to tell anyone, even me. She said she'd wanted to tell me for a long time, but figured it was best if it came from my parents." Annie sighed. "I went home and confronted my mom and dad. I think they're still in a bit of shock. They didn't have any time to prepare for how they'd tell me."

"Seems they had over twenty years to prepare," Grandma mumbled.

Ian cleared his throat. "I'm not sure what I can do to help you. I can't take this case pro bono."

"You mean for free?" Annie frowned.

Grandma reached over and smacked him on the shoulder. "Let her pay as she goes."

He shot his grandmother a dirty look, which she returned with glaring eyes and pursed lips.

Ian turned back around toward Annie. Her eyes sparkled with a glimmer of hope. As much as he wanted to, he couldn't do this for free. He needed the money to run the agency, not to mention pay his own bills. But something compelled him to help her.

Then a thought came to him. "Have you ever had any experience caring for children?" Ian glanced over his shoulder toward his grandmother, and added, "Or adults?"

"Huh?" Annie blinked. She looked like a deer caught in headlights. "I helped take care of my grandmother . . . before she died."

"Died?" Ian swallowed the lump in his throat. Maybe his idea wasn't as good as he thought.

"She had cancer."

Ian suppressed a sigh of relief.

"I've got a solution to both our problems." He covered his mouth and coughed. He didn't mean to refer to his grandmother as a problem. But she needed care—care he couldn't give her and work at the same time. "I need a live-in helper to look after my grandmother. She's a brittle diabetic and she needs someone around to monitor her blood sugar. If you agree to take care of her, I'll research your case in exchange. What do you say?"

Impulsively, he bit his lower lip. He didn't know if he wanted her to say yes or no. He needed to get work done and it proved to be a challenge with his grandmother tailgating him all day. But Annie's gorgeous brown eyes would distract him to no end. Either way he was doomed.

"It would give me a place to stay instead of the hotel." Annie frowned. The way she stared off into space, Ian could tell she was deep in thought, probably weighing her options. Her lips slowly eased into a smile. "Okay."

Ian knew his ship had sunk when his grandmother cheered. This couldn't be good. His grandmother had already devoured six live-in helpers. There had to be an ulterior motive behind her sudden compliance.

"I'll need a couple references." Ian handed a blank piece of paper across the desk to Annie. "People who can vouch for you."

Annie nodded. She took the paper and smiled as she grabbed a pen out of the cup holder on his desk. "Thank you."

He didn't have a prayer. Between Annie's smile, and Grandma's sudden pliability, he had the feeling he was headed for the guillotine with no escape.

Annie handed back the paper. He scanned the three names, one of which was a pastor.

"Let me do a background check and call these references. Then I'll get back in touch with you later today." Ian smiled as he pushed to his feet, extending his hand.

She stood and shook his hand. "Sounds wonderful. Thanks."

After Annie left, Ian picked up the phone and dialed a friend from the precinct.

Jason answered on the third ring. "Hey, buddy, what can I do for you?"

"I need a favor." Ian laughed. He knew Jason expected as much whenever he called. It was usually why he called his friend. "I need you to find out all you can about an adoption agency and while you're at it, find out all you can

140

on Annie Spelman. I need the latter ASAP. And while you're at it, check out her adoptive parents. I'll fax you over the information."

Other Books by Susette Williams:

Mail Order Brides novelette series ~
JESSIE'S BRIDE –Book 1
MONTANA'S BRIDE –Book 2
CALEB'S BRIDE –Book 3
MARSHALL'S BRIDE–Book 4
HUSBAND OF THE BRIDE–Book 5

Texas Wildflowers novelette series ~
FREE TO LOVE –Book 1
FREE TO HEAL –Book 2
FREE TO PROTECT –Book 3
FREE TO SERVE –Book 4
FREE TO ROAM –Book 5
FREE TO FORGIVE –Book 6

The Amish Ways novelette series ~
THE WIDOWER'S NEW WIFE –Book 1
ROAD TO REDEMPTION –Book 2

Seasons of the Heart novella series ~
FALLING IN LOVE – Book 1
WINTER CHILL – Book 2
SPRING BREAK – Book 3
HEATED SUMMER – Book 4

Maid for Murder series ~
Maid for Murder: DEADLY BUSINESS – Book 1
Maid for Murder: DEADLY CONFESSIONS – Book 2

Novellas ~
ACCIDENTAL MEETING
SCROOGE FALLS IN LOVE – Typecast Christmas series
SHADOWS OF DOUBT
MORE THAN FRIENDS
LITTLE ORPHAN ANNIE

Novels ~
SOMETHING ABOUT SAM
HONORABLE INTENTIONS

Please visit my website to sign up for my newsletter so that you can receive information about new releases, contests and giveaways.

Author Website: www.susettewilliams.com

Made in the USA
Columbia, SC
20 January 2020